D1540323

LONEWILD
Winter

A Wentworth Cove Novel: Book 3

Rebecca Stevenson

Dedication

To my brother James—my rock, my hero

Contents

Chapter One

Lonewild, though empty and silent now, stood proud and majestic atop Bender's Bluff as it had for nine decades, and Reagan Hart thought it absolutely perfect for her and her daughter Meredith. The house was almost completely surrounded by sixty-foot-tall Eastern White Pine trees. Only from the Atlantic Ocean could someone get a glimpse of the solarium running the length of the structure's first floor.

"I'll take it," Reagan told Samantha Evans.

"Don't you want to see the inside?" the realtor asked. "I mean, I'm not one to turn down a deal, but my clients usually want to see the whole property before signing a contract."

"Of course, but I'll take it. I'm sure of that." Reagan shifted her weight to the other foot, eager to get on with the matter at hand.

"It might be hard for people to find you here unless they know where they're going. As you noticed, it can't be seen from the road, and I doubt many people will be coming to visit by boat."

"That's what makes it perfect for us." Reagan fidgeted with her car keys, thankful she had decided to follow the realtor instead of trying to find the house herself. How had she lucked into this place? She would be forever in David's debt for telling her about it when she confidentially revealed to him and Elizabeth her intention to move to Wentworth Cove. Standing no more than three feet away from the front door, she was able to survey the front yard. Having a yard to care for would be unlike anything she was used to, but in the spring, she thought, it might be fun to plant red geraniums along the edge of the house...and herbs in the back, lots of herbs.

"Ida Carter cherished Lonewild. I told her it was no use putting up a sign, so we decided to advertise by word-of-mouth. That's not the way we usually do things at Evans Realty, but then Miss Carter is not your usual landlady. I imagine you'll find that out soon enough, if not in person, from talk around town. That is, if you're planning to stay for a while...which I suppose you are if you're signing a twelve-month lease. You heard about it from David Norsworthy at the art gallery? I think that's what my assistant said."

"Yes." *Could we just get on with it, and would you please quit prying?* Reagan was beginning to feel uneasy with this talkative realtor.

"Would you and your daughter like to take a quick tour now? Marjorie, was it?" Samantha smiled at the young girl standing somewhat behind her mother.

"Meredith," Reagan and her twelve-year-old daughter said in unison.

"Well, Meredith, I suppose you'll be enrolling in school soon and meeting some of the young people in Wentworth Cove. What grade are you in?"

Meredith glanced at her mother who nodded her consent. "Seventh. Mom, aren't you going to homeschool me?" she asked. "That's what you said."

"We'll have to wait and see if I have time. Could we have that tour now? I have a moving van arriving this afternoon and I'm kind of in a time crunch."

"Oh, my. You do work fast. Let's go and then we can head back to the office and sign the papers—that is, if you still want it after you see the inside."

"I will."

There were only a few things Reagan Hart was sure of at this juncture. Leasing this out-of-the-way property was one of them. Here she and Meredith could relax in the safety of stately pines and not fear being seen by passersby. They could come and go in the anonymity of their new car and begin their lives anew. So why did she still have that sensation in the pit of her stomach? The one she first felt when she received the news that Jared would soon be out of prison?

"Okay, then. This is the fastest deal I've made since I've been in the real estate business. It's been on the market only a week. That's when Miss Carter went into that assisted living facility in Kennebunk…a week ago yesterday. We had no idea it would rent this fast, but I'm sure she needs the money. Those places aren't cheap, you know. My mother-in-law was in one for seven years. Nearly cleaned her out. My husband was afraid he was going to have to get a job to help her pay the expenses, but she passed before he had to."

Reagan could have been mistaken, but she thought she detected a look of relief on the woman's face. "Could we see the inside now?"

"Oh sure. Come on. What are we waiting for?"

Reagan sighed. *What are we waiting for, indeed.*

"Cool!" Meredith said as she stepped across the threshold and spied the vintage wallpaper with pink and red roses. On one side of the room were built-in

3

bookshelves with beveled glass doors and finely carved woodwork on either side of a marble mantel. Meredith looked up at the ornate ceiling that housed a crystal chandelier. She waltzed over, smiling inwardly at creaking floorboards, and ran her hand over the dark wood trim that outlined the arched opening between the living and dining rooms. "Mom, don't you just love it?"

Reagan had seen houses like this in movies, but the thought of ever living in one had never crossed her mind. It bore little resemblance to their contemporary apartment in New York City. "It's nice, Mere. Not exactly what we're used to…but nice. It will work for us. At least it's clean."

"Clean? It's *heavenly*."

It wasn't supposed to be like this. Jared and Reagan and Meredith were supposed to live in New York City for the rest of their lives. But life had dealt them—actually Jared had dealt them—a different hand when he had made the decision that turned their lives upside down. Now here they were in Maine, she and Meredith. Jared would be out of prison soon—as if nothing had happened—except that he wouldn't have his family. And Reagan wondered how he'd take their leaving. If her instincts were right, he wouldn't be any too happy about it.

Back at the realty office, Reagan had skimmed and signed the contract, thankful she trusted David not to send her to a place with a landlord she might have to question—or one who might question her—and a contract she'd have to read thoroughly. Lonewild was private, affordable, and available immediately. That was all she was concerned with. Get in. Get settled. Get on with her life.

"My only job was to get the place rented to someone who would, as Miss Carter insisted, love it and take care of it. I felt comfortable showing it to you since you were recommended by David Norsworthy. Have you known him a long time?" Samantha Evans asked.

"About five years."

"You'll take your check every month to Miss Carter herself at Sundown Assisted Living Center in Kennebunk. It's just—"

"I'm sure I can find it." Reagan said, reaching out to shake Samantha's hand. "Now if you'll just give me the house key..."

"Oh, of course. That would help, wouldn't it? Here you go. She'll be expecting the first month's rent on Monday or Tuesday. I suggested you could mail it, but she insisted on meeting you in person. That's Miss Carter's way. Oh, well. You'll see for yourself soon. If you have any questions—"

"I'll call. Thanks. I'd better get back before my moving van arrives," Reagan explained as she started backing out the door.

"I noticed you have New York plates on your car. From the city?"

"Um..." Reagan resisted the urge to roll her eyes, opting to stall instead. She didn't owe Samantha Evans any explanations.

"Oh, that's okay. My husband says I'm too nosy. But he also says I talk too much, so I don't put much stock in what he says. A realtor has to get to know people to have a sense of what types of properties to show them, right? You... You were easy. I just took a cue from David when he told Andrea you'd probably be interested in Lonewild. Anyway, I'm sure I'll see you around. Enjoy your new home."

"I think I'd like her husband," Meredith said when they were back in the car.

"What? Whose husband?" Reagan's mind was on a thousand different things—getting back in time to meet the moving van, stocking up on groceries, deciding what to do about the rest of the school year for Meredith, finding a

5

job. She knew the money she had in savings wouldn't last forever. And she knew she didn't earn enough on her watercolors to support her and her daughter. She'd left a part time job in a busy art gallery in New York City, but David and Elizabeth didn't have enough business to support hiring her. They'd promised to keep their eyes and ears open for her, though. There were some galleries in Kennebunkport. They'd ask around.

"That real estate lady. I think I'd like her husband," Meredith said, interrupting her mother's thoughts.

"What makes you say that?"

"Well, I know he's smart and I like smart people."

"You know he's... *How* do you know he's smart?"

"She *is* nosy, and she *does* talk too much."

Reagan had to smile at her daughter. While she was taking care of the details of their new lives, Meredith was sizing people up as she always did.

"Yep. He must be a pretty smart guy, huh? I wonder why he doesn't have a job."

"Now who's getting nosy, Mom?"

Darn that girl, Reagan thought. *Nothing gets past her.*

Chapter Two

After seven years and five months of confinement, Jared Loper walked out of the Federal Correctional Institution two hours north of New York City—a free man. Free in one sense of the word, but with a parole officer instead of a medical license, the former anesthesiologist was unsure of the future. Unsure in a generic sense, but he was certain of one thing: He would get his daughter back no matter what it took.

His wife of six years had divorced him and gained full custody of their five-year-old daughter as soon as his trial was over and the jury foreman had said, "We find the defendant guilty, Your Honor." He hadn't seen Meredith since his arrest. Reagan had made sure of that, and the custody decree awarded him no visitation rights.

It would have been senseless to try to call his ex-wife when he got out. She had chosen not to visit him either…although the prison was only two hours from the city. But he needed a ride and he needed a place to stay, so he'd called the only person who had consistently kept in touch.

"It's great to see you on this side of the fence." Henry Loper got out the car and hugged his son. "I wish Mom was here to celebrate this day with us. But she had faith that you'd be out before your sentence was up. She prayed for you every day, you know."

"She had more faith than I did. One of my two biggest regrets was not being able to go to her memorial service."

"And your other one?"

"Losing Reagan and Meredith, of course. Have you seen them lately?"

Henry had dreaded this part of Jared's release from prison. He'd have to be told, and Henry knew he would have to be the one to do it. "They were over a couple of weeks ago, but I have some news that I don't look forward to telling you...especially on this happy day."

"Go ahead. I have a feeling I know what it is. They don't want to see me at all, do they? Reagan has poisoned Meredith's mind about me, hasn't she?"

If only it were that simple, Henry thought as he took a step toward his son. "I don't know about that, but they're gone, Jared."

Jared stepped back and bristled. "Gone? Gone where?"

"That's just it," Henry said. "No one knows. Reagan wouldn't tell me. Said they were going to make a new life for themselves. I think she knew you would try to get partial custody, and she wants to keep Meredith away from you. Your daughter has grown into a beautiful young lady, Jared. And sweet. And smart. You'd be proud of her. Reagan has done a good job. It hasn't been easy on her."

"It hasn't been easy on *her*? What do you think I've been going through?" Jared shouted.

"Don't raise your voice to me, son. I love you and I will support you until you can get back on your feet, but don't think for one minute that I've forgotten what you did to cause this heartache."

Although Jared's medical practice had provided him a substantial salary, he'd wanted more. And that desire had given way to temptation when some of his wealthier patients expressed the "need" for more pain medication than the amount required for their treatment and were willing to fork over big bucks to get it.

When one of his patients died of an oxycodone overdose, the district attorney began a probe into the matter and found others who had overdosed, recovered, and were willing to talk. On assurance of immunity, three of Dr. Loper's former patients testified at his trial, telling the jury they'd been able to obtain any kind of opioid they wanted with a significant amount of under-the-table cash.

"I served my time," Jared countered. "Are you going to keep bringing it up? Because if you are, there are other places I can stay."

"I'm not going to keep bringing it up, but you have to understand that you lost Reagan's trust. And it's going to take more than getting out of prison a few years early to gain it back."

"On good behavior…"

"Yes. On good behavior. I know you've done everything you could to regain the trust of your friends and family. But it's going to take more time for some people than others."

"I know Reagan can be stubborn."

"She's stubborn about protecting her daughter."

"*Our* daughter," Jared reminded him, raising his voice again. "Whose side are you on?"

"*Your* daughter. I'm on the side of understanding why people do some of the things they do. One of the perks that comes with being a psychologist, I guess."

"I'll call Al as soon as we get home. I'm sure he'll let me bunk on his couch for a while. Seems like I've already worn out my welcome with you."

"That's crazy talk. Of course you'll stay with me. I just think we should be able to be completely honest and transparent with each other. Haven't I always taught you that's the sign of a good relationship?"

"Is that your underhanded way of saying I deserved what I got because I wasn't honest and transparent with Reagan?"

"Maybe you'd better call Al." Henry handed Jared his phone. "Do you know his number?"

After a couple of minutes of internet searching, Jared found his old friend's number and dialed.

"Al, buddy. It's—"

"Jared. Good to hear your voice, man. You're out, right?"

"I'm out. Be back in the city in a couple of hours. Listen—"

"You need a place to crash."

"I was planning to stay with my dad, but—" Jared said, hoping Al would remember the strain the trial had put on their relationship and understand his reluctance to stay with his dad.

"Don't give it a second thought. Of course you can bunk with me. Just me and Felix over here. We'd welcome the company."

"Felix?"

"I didn't tell you about him last time I was up for a visit? I guess that's been a while. Sorry I didn't come more often, buddy. He's a Rottweiler…but not scary at all. Of course, he might lick you to death."

"Great. Listen, I appreciate—"

"No problem. I'm in the same bachelor pad. You remember how to get here?"

"Sure. I'll just get a taxi. You be home in a couple of hours?"

"Yep. Is Reagan—"

"She's gone…or so my dad says. He could be covering for her, though." Jared rounded the corner of the building to finish his conversation out of earshot of his dad. "I wouldn't put it past him. Claims he doesn't know where she is. But I can't imagine she would just up and leave

10

without giving him any hope of ever seeing Meredith again. But, hey. I'll fill you in when I get there."

Jared walked back around the corner and tossed his dad's phone to him. The drive home was quiet. Two excruciatingly long hours.

When they reached the city, Jared said a quick goodbye, grabbed his duffel, and headed out to the sidewalk to grab a cab. He knew his dad would have taken him to Al's place, but about all he had left was his pride and he wasn't about to lose that after being out of prison for only a few hours. Humility was overrated, he thought, and he refused to humble himself to his father...or anyone else, for that matter. He wasn't exactly proud of what he had done, but he didn't think it was so bad either. Didn't he supply people with medicine they needed? Was it his fault if they chose to use it unwisely?

A cab approached and Jared threw his hand in the air to hail it.

Jared exited the taxi and made his way up to the third floor of Al's apartment building. Apartment 301 if he remembered correctly. If not, surely someone on this floor would know Al and be able to point Jared in the direction of his place. He located 301 and knocked lightly. Hadn't Al mentioned having a Rottweiler now? Jared didn't want to put him into a barking frenzy.

Al slung open the door and pulled Jared into a bear hug. "Hey, man. How does it feel? Stupid question, huh?"

"Mixed feelings," Jared answered as he reached down to pet Felix. Al was right. He *could* lick a person to death. "Great to be out, of course, but—"

"There's a *but*? Come in. Come in, buddy. Lemme take your things. Sit... Sorry. I'm used to talking to the dog. Still the anti-social recluse you knew in med school. Have a seat. Or are you tired of sitting? Want a beer?"

"First time I've heard that question in a while. Sure." Jared took the opportunity to look around the room when Al went into the kitchen. The apartment was much like he remembered it but with nicer furniture. How could he still afford this place and all this new furniture? He wasn't practicing medicine. He'd told Jared he was a day trader and enjoyed being his own boss and making his own work schedule. *Maybe that's something I should look into,* Jared thought. *Gotta do something outside the medical field.*

"You were saying?" Al asked when he came back, two beers in hand. "Apparently there's a *but*."

"There's more than one *but*. First, I can't practice medicine anymore. So—"

"Oh, that. As you know, I haven't practiced medicine for six years and I'm doing okay. What's the other one? I'm guessing it has to do with Reagan and the kid. What was her name?"

"Meredith." Jared vividly remembered looking through the book of baby names with Reagan. If he liked one, she didn't. If she liked one, he didn't. But by the time they got to the *M*s, they were ready to agree, and Meredith it was. Just saying the name gave him a fresh longing to see his daughter. "Yeah. It has everything to do with them. They're gone."

"Gone? As in *left New York?*

"Yeah, as in left New York and I don't have any idea where they went. That ex-wife of mine took my daughter and vanished. My dad doesn't even know where they are. At least that's what he's saying."

"You gonna look for them?"

"Of course I'm going to look for them. I'm going to find them, too, if it's the last thing I do. She has no right to take my daughter away from me."

"No right? So she kidnapped her? You can take that to court, can't you?"

"Not exactly. She has full custody." Jared shot to his feet and started pacing.

"But you still have rights. You're not going to take this lying down, are you?"

"Actually, I don't have rights—legally, that is. Reagan hired a top-notch attorney who managed to convince the judge—a woman, wouldn't you know—that I was an unfit father because I slipped up once and took Mere with me on one delivery. One. I thought she was too young at four to know—or care or even remember—what was going on, but apparently I underestimated my daughter. Guess she got her brains from me." Jared gave a sardonic half laugh. "More than likely she was coached by the attorney about what to say to the judge, but of course I can't prove that. Anyway, the judge said it wasn't in the 'best interest of the child' for her to continue to see me and awarded full custody to Reagan."

"So that means that Reagan has every right to leave New York and not let you know where she is."

Jared sat back down and pounded his fist on the coffee table. "That's my kid," he said, his voice growing louder. "She has my DNA. I have every right in the world to see my own kid. I don't care what some black-robed feminist has to say. You know female judges always rule in favor of the mother. I'll bet Reagan's attorney managed to get the case tried in that judge's courtroom. Probably paid her off or something."

"You see everything in terms of dollar signs, don't you? Isn't that what got you in trouble in the first place?"

"Okay, Al. Just tell me if you don't want me here. My dad essentially said he didn't want me staying with him. That's why I came here. Thought I could count on you. Guess not. If you feel that way, just tell me to leave."

"No, buddy," Al assured him. "You can stay here until you get back on your feet. But just know that I'm not going to walk on eggshells around you. I call it as I see it. Always have. Always will. If you'll recall, that's why I never enjoyed the medical field. Couldn't keep from speaking my mind during my residency."

"I do remember that. Admired you for it, actually. So you'll tell me if you want me to leave?"

"I'll tell you. And I won't pull any punches. In fact, I'm telling you right now that I don't think you should try to find Reagan and Meredith, but…that's your business. What are your plans? Now that you've lost your license, I mean?"

Jared remembered that Al always did cut to the chase. "I've done some research. Thought about selling medical equipment. There's money to be made there, I think. I'll just have to find a company that'll take a chance on an ex-con. Ex-con. That doesn't roll off the tongue easily. I hate the way it sounds."

"Well, actions have consequences."

"Don't start—"

"I told you I'm gonna call it as I see it, and as long as you're staying with me—"

"Fair enough. Where should I park my bag?" Jared asked, looking around.

"Right there by the couch. This place don't have a guest suite."

Jared didn't mind sleeping on Al's couch. If he'd gone home with his dad, he would have had a nice, comfortable bed in his old room. But, he rationalized, he'd trade a bed for his pride any day of the week.

Chapter Three

Reagan and Meredith hadn't been back at Lonewild ten minutes when Reagan looked at her ringing phone and saw Elizabeth Norsworthy's name pop up. *Ah, the comfort of caller ID*, she thought, answering it.

"Reagan? It's Elizabeth. David and I heard you rented Lonewild and were wondering if you need any help moving in. Are you planning to stay there tonight? Is your furniture here yet?"

They already heard she rented Lonewild? It might be more of an adjustment than she thought moving from a big city to a small town. Did she want everyone knowing her business? Well, they were here now and time would tell if it had been the right move.

"It should be here in about an hour, and yes, we'll stay here tonight. The movers will set up our beds for us. How did you hear…? Oh, I suppose Samantha Evans came by the gallery."

"David ran into her at Lobster Bistro. By the time he got away, our food was cold," Elizabeth said, laughing.

Note to self, Reagan thought. *Keep as much personal information from Samantha Evans as possible.*

"Elizabeth, the fewer people who know we're here, the better. I realize we're a long way from New York City up here on the Maine coast, but you know what I mean."

"I do, but this is a small, tight-knit community. Everyone knows just about everything about everyone else here, but they don't talk about Cove people outside the community. I think this is the best decision you could have made…considering the circumstances. How's Meredith?"

"She's adjusting better than I expected. I think she's looking on this as an adventure. I just hope it's not more of an adventure than we would like. I was thinking about homeschooling her, but she wants to go to school to meet some friends. She had to leave some very good girlfriends back in the city. What do you think? Would it be safe? Also, I'll probably have to get a job at some point."

"I think it'll be all right if you talk with the middle school principal and tell him no one can pick her up but you—or someone else you delegate, like me. My school is only a couple of blocks away from the middle school and I'd be happy to bring her home anytime you're tied up. We're empty nesters now that Jessica's in college. It's a strange feeling. Oh, I almost forgot what I called about. David and I were wondering if you and Meredith could come to our house for dinner tonight."

"That's so sweet of you, but we'll have our furniture and boxes by then and we'd like to start setting up the house. Lonewild is perfect for us, by the way. Tell David thanks for thinking of it. And what a perfect name. It really fits this place."

Reagan thought of the house as a large peephole. She could look out at the ocean through any east-facing window and at the driveway that ran up to the front entrance from any west-facing window. But a person would have to be extremely close to the house to see it from either direction. It seemed a lifetime away from New

York City. And that suited Reagan because she felt she and Meredith were worlds removed from their life there.

"Lonewild has been a Wentworth Cove icon for as long as I've lived here. Miss Carter named it, I think. She's lived there forever," Elizabeth said. "Then can I bring something over for you? I won't stay. I'll just drop it off and leave…or stay and help you unpack. Whichever would be more helpful."

"I've lived in New York City all my life. Is this what small-town hospitality is like for real? I've only read about it and thought it was pure fiction."

"I can't speak for all small towns, but I think you'll find Wentworth Cove friendly."

On one hand Reagan craved friendly people. She wanted to be accepted here, wanted Meredith to have as many friends as she did in the city. On the other hand, she needed to maintain their privacy. Jared would be out of prison any day now, and she wasn't sure taking her mother's maiden name would be enough to protect them. "Food would be welcome. I haven't located a market yet. Is there one here, or will I have to go into Kennebunk?"

"I think you'll like Carson's Market on Shore Road. You can get almost everything you'll need there. I'm slow-cooking a pot roast with carrots and potatoes for tonight. I'll bring you some around six. How does that sound?"

"Too good to be true. We'll be here. Thanks again, Elizabeth. I'll definitely owe you and David."

"I'll tell you how you can return the favor. We sold two of your watercolors last week. We could use a couple more for your collection. Our website has been getting a lot of hits, and our online business is really picking up."

"Give me a couple of days to unpack and see what I have. I hope to start painting again as soon as we're settled in. Do you remember which two you sold?"

"Yes. One was of colorful sailboats in a harbor, and the other was the stone church in Kennebunkport out by Walker's Point."

"Good. That helps me to know what's selling. I can't wait to explore and find some more local places to paint."

As Reagan put her phone down, she began to feel anxious at the thought of going to the market to buy groceries. And the thought of Meredith away from her in a new school. Yes, she'd toyed with the idea of homeschooling, but her funds wouldn't last forever, and her painting wouldn't cover the bills completely, so she would probably have to get a job—at least part time. Ryan had offered to help, and he was certainly more than able, but she wanted to make it on her own.

Since they'd been small, she and Ryan had been as competitive as any twins who adored each other could be. At seven, she was determined to be as good at ice-skating as he was. When he started playing hockey at twelve, she excelled at figure skating with an eye on the Olympics and spent every waking moment outside of school taking lessons from a coach who had trained several Olympic medal winners.

They were competitive academically, too, with Ryan graduating valedictorian of their small private school and Reagan taking salutatorian honors. She missed beating him by four-tenths of a point, but she was happy for him. Their competition never created animosity. They always celebrated each other's accomplishments.

He'd been her rock these last seven years. Although his architectural firm was based in Boston, he traveled to New York City at least once a month to confer with prospective clients and check in on his sister and niece.

A knock on the door interrupted Reagan's thoughts. "Mom," Meredith called from the kitchen. "I think it's the movers."

"Let me get it. I want you to stay upstairs while they're unloading the furniture," Reagan answered her daughter. The fewer people who knew about her, the better. Reagan was sure of that. *I know I can't hide her from everyone forever, but I can be cautious*, she thought as she peered out the peephole in the front door at a man, short and stocky. *I'll bet he could lift a refrigerator by himself,* Reagan mused, eyeing the muscles that bulged through his T-shirt.

"Good heavens, lady. You're about as far from New York City as you could get. It's a good thing my GPS worked out here in the boonies. How will anyone ever find this place? How did *you* find this place?"

"Could you just start bringing in the furniture and boxes? I'm in kind of a hurry."

"Sure. We can do that. Come on, Jeff. But I don't know why you're in such a hurry. There's no place to go when you get moved in. Gonna be quite an adjustment for you, I'm afraid."

"Yeah. Well. That'll be my problem, won't it?" Reagan wasn't usually short with people, but her nerves were on edge, and she didn't want Meredith to have to stay upstairs for hours. "Could we get the kitchen boxes first so I can be unpacking them while you bring in the things for the living room and two downstairs bedrooms? My bedroom and a guest bedroom. Nothing goes upstairs."

"Sure is a big house for only one person. Jeff," he shouted over his shoulder, "lady wants the kitchen boxes first."

"Mom, you won't believe what I found upstairs," Meredith said as soon as the movers were gone and the coast was clear.

"I know Miss Carter left some of her furniture. I think someone's going to take it or sell it soon, so don't get attached to anything." Reagan had to laugh at her daughter. For a twelve-year-old, she had a more-than-mild attraction to old things—old buildings, old ships, old books, old people, and apparently this old house.

"She's an old soul herself," Ryan had often said of his niece.

That's because she had to grow up too fast, Reagan thought.

"I'm not getting attached," Meredith replied, "but I'm telling you, you won't believe it."

"Okay, I'll check it out later. Right now let's get the downstairs put together. Why don't you work on your bedroom while I unpack kitchen boxes? Elizabeth will be here with dinner soon."

"All right, but I'm telling you now, Mom, you won't believe it."

"No? Well, I guess I could expect just about anything in a house this old."

"I know. Isn't it wonderful? Did you know that you can open the windows upstairs and hear the ocean? Could I move my bedroom up there? Please?"

Reagan would have liked nothing better than to let Meredith move upstairs and turn the second downstairs bedroom into a studio. The room had a southern exposure, and she had almost drooled when she'd seen the way the sun streamed in on a cool fall day. In the winter, the rays would be even more welcome and lovely.

"You know we're supposed to occupy only the downstairs. I don't think Miss Carter would be happy if she knew you'd been looking around up there. So why don't you just stay down here unless someone we don't know comes to the door. Deal?"

"But that takes all the fun out of this adventure. How long am I gonna have to stay locked up?"

"Oh, Mere, you're not locked up. We're just being cautious. I thought we agreed this move was for the best. We couldn't have stayed in New York. You know that, right?"

"Okay then. If I'm not locked up, can I go to school? I'll be as safe there as I am here," Meredith said, her eyes helping plead her case.

Reagan kissed her daughter on the top of her head. "That's one thing I want to talk to Elizabeth about when she comes over. She teaches at Kennebunk Elementary.

The middle school is close, I think. She offered to give you a ride home when I'm not able to pick you up."

"There. It's all set then. How 'bout Monday? Can we go Monday? I can't even tell Maisie and Kelsey where I am when I FaceTime them. What fun is that?"

"We'll see. I know you'll be bored stuck here in the house. I might have to get a part time job, too, and I guess you'll be safer at school than here alone while I'm working."

Reagan flinched at the sound of the doorbell and Meredith asked, "Want me to go upstairs?"

Reagan peered out the front-door peephole again. "No. It's Elizabeth," she answered, opening the door to her friend. "Hi. You're a welcome sight. Mere, let's give Elizabeth a hand with these things."

Reagan had met Elizabeth and David Norsworthy when she ventured up to Maine on a painting and selling trip a few years ago. They had welcomed both her and her paintings and had since sold many of them in their gallery. But theirs was not only a business relationship. They'd become friends and were some of the only people she could trust with the news of her need to get out of the city.

"Sure. Hi, Mrs. Norsworthy," Meredith said.

"Hi, Meredith. Welcome to Wentworth Cove. And you can call me Elizabeth now that you're living here. My third graders are the only ones who call me Mrs. Norsworthy. It's a mouthful. Helping your mom get unpacked?"

"A little bit, but I've mostly been—"

"She's a great help," Reagan interrupted, cutting her eyes at her daughter. "When she doesn't get distracted, that is. Let's put these things in the kitchen."

"I'd forgotten how cool this house is. I don't think I've been inside since I came with David to see Brett once when he was in town for a few weeks. But that was some years ago."

"Brett?" Reagan asked.

21

"He's Miss Carter's nephew. Well, great nephew, I guess. Her only living relative now that his parents and grandparents are gone. He helped her get settled into the assisted living facility, and I suppose he'll be the one to finish moving her things out. But he lives in Augusta, so it might take a while. I hope they're not in your way."

"No. They're not in—" Meredith started.

"They're fine. We'll be occupying the downstairs. It's plenty of room for us."

"I don't want to keep you from unpacking. I'll text you directions to Carson's Market so you can stock up tomorrow. Could I help with anything before I go?" Elizabeth asked.

"This food is such a huge help. You and David have been our salvation. I couldn't imagine any place better than Wentworth Cove for our situation, and Lonewild is perfect. It's like it was made for us—and the timing—with Miss Carter moving out a week ago. I guess we're meant to be here. I think I'm feeling better about the school thing too. I'll enroll her Monday."

"You will? Thanks, Mom!" Meredith threw her arms around her mother.

"And thanks again for the food, Elizabeth," Reagan said. "We'll have this unpacking done in a couple of days. Tell David I'll come by the gallery one day next week."

After a day and a half of lining shelves and putting things away and moving furniture and hanging pictures, Monday finally arrived along with a late October frost and snow flurries. Reagan had promised to take Meredith to the middle school in Kennebunk and at least check it out, meet the principal, and assess its safety factor. True to her word, she'd set her clock for six-fifteen and when it sounded she awoke to the welcome aroma of coffee coming from the kitchen.

"Meredith? What are you doing up already? I thought I'd have to wake you. It's still dark outside."

"Are you kidding? I set my alarm for six. This is the first day of the rest of my life. I heard Uncle Ryan say that once, but today really feels like that. Have you seen the snow?" Meredith asked, opening the curtain to reveal the flood of moonlight illuminating the falling flakes.

"Nice, huh? Just enough light to see some flurries. I wonder what time sunrise is here. We're quite a bit farther east than we were in the city. Guess I'd better check the weather on my phone since I'm not used to driving on these roads." Though the room was warm, Reagan felt an uneasy chill as thoughts of Jared flitted through her mind. But she wasn't about to ruin this day for Meredith, so she quickly regained her composure by trying to erase the last seven years from her mind.

"I can't wait to see what the kids are like up here." Meredith's excitement was palpable. "Do you think they'll be like my friends in New York? Do you think they'll like me?"

"Of course they will. You just be your sweet self and before long I'm sure you'll have more friends than you know what to do with. Scrambled eggs?"

"You brought eggs? I thought you just brought coffee and granola bars in the car."

"What am I thinking? No, we don't have eggs. I'll get some today. How about a granola bar then?"

"You know what I'd like for breakfast?"

"What?"

"A granola bar."

"I think I can manage that. Thanks for getting the coffee started. Looks like a few more light flurries today. Probably not enough to get the snowplows out. Let's get dressed and get you to school before the roads get icy."

"I'll be ready in fifteen minutes. I already have my outfit picked out," Meredith said, her eyes filled with expectation.

"Why am I not surprised?" Meredith had always stood out in school, not only soaking in what her teachers presented and earning high grades, but also making friends. She'd had to leave her two best friends behind, but she was well liked enough by the rest of the students in her class to be voted class president for both her fifth and sixth grade years. Reagan hoped the kids here would be as accepting and school would continue to be a positive experience for her daughter.

Chapter Four

"Morning, Aunt Ida." Brett Mason had driven the hour and a half from Augusta to Kennebunk, and as he'd suspected, he found his aunt sitting in the front gathering room of Sundown Assisted Living Center. He imagined she was facing the door so she could greet any prospective residents who might walk in. She'd probably already met all the current residents and staff and given them her take on the place and was ready to start on the new souls who would likely need her advice.

Ida Carter was known in the Cove as an outspoken octogenarian, but when people needed a little common sense advice, it seemed all roads led to Lonewild. No doubt she would keep Sundown hopping with visitors. In fact, she'd already considered petitioning the owners to change the name to Sunrise. Or at the very least, Sunshine. "Sundown? For a retirement home? Are you kidding?" she'd commented to her nephew when he'd first driven her over to look at it.

"Oh, Brett. I'm so happy to see you. What are you doing here though?" Ida asked, eyeing him speculatively, one eyebrow raised. "Did you lose your job?"

"No, Aunt Ida," Brett answered, chuckling and pulling up a chair beside her. "Still gainfully employed at *Augusta Tribune*. I had an assignment out at Walker's Point and decided to take a couple of days before and after to get some things settled at Lonewild."

"It's leased, you know. There's really nothing you have to do now."

Brett's eyes widened. "What do you mean, it's leased? Already?" He raised his voice. "What about the things we left upstairs?"

"Calm down. They're using the downstairs only. Samantha said David recommended them, so I wasn't worried."

"They? Have you met them? You're too trusting, you know."

"David's your friend. Don't you trust him?"

Brett shifted slightly in his chair. "Of course I trust David, but he's not the one who's living there. He's not the one whose treasures are still upstairs. Those people could steal you blind."

"For a journalist, you sure can choose inappropriate words to express yourself." Ida Carter shot her nephew a gentle glance. "Wouldn't be much of a loss would it, my eyesight?"

"I'm so sorry, Aunt Ida. I haven't gotten used to it yet. You stay on top of things so much better than most people, it's hard to remember you've lost a lot of your vision."

"Then you've forgotten why I left my precious Lonewild in the first place. I didn't want to, you know. But that's all right. I wasn't fussing at you. Don't know what I'd do without you." She patted her nephew's strong, masculine hand with her thin, weathered one.

"How are you doing, Aunt Ida? Are you happy here? I know it's not Lonewild, but it seems nice. Three meals a day. People to talk to. A nice apartment. You okay?" He sincerely hoped she was. The only alternative was to take her to Augusta to live with him and turn his office into a bedroom. She'd be gone in a month if she had to live that far from Lonewild and all the Cove people who relied on her sage advice, he thought.

"I'm fine, honey. I learned a long time ago that you take your happiness with you wherever you go. Some people haven't brought their happiness here, but I'm working on them," she said, smiling.

"I'll bet you are." Brett laughed at his aunt's honesty. He thought she always looked a bit younger when she smiled. The wrinkles at the outer edges of her eyes were smile lines now, not crow's feet. Then his look took a sudden serious turn. "I'm concerned with all those things upstairs at Lonewild."

"Those things? Keep them. Sell them. Give them away. They're no good to me now, and I don't know why you're worried about them."

"You know what I mean. What do you want me to do with—"

"Throw them away, Brett. You shouldn't have to be bothered with them…and neither should the people who are renting Lonewild."

"I'm not going to throw them away. Let me take them to—"

"No. We've already been over this. I don't want them there. David wouldn't want them there. Take them to your house then if you don't want to throw them away. Or…you could sell them, use the proceeds to retire and buy a villa in the South of France." Ida threw her head back and laughed that hearty laugh she was famous for.

"Whatever you say. How can I get in touch with the people who moved in so that I can coordinate cleaning out the upstairs? I guess I'll take most of the things to

Goodwill...or see if they'll pick it up. That would be easier. Some things I'll take to Augusta."

"You could probably get her name from David. I haven't met her, but Samantha said it's a woman and a little girl. Says she's nice but a little mysterious."

"Mysterious? Then I know we need to get your things out of the house. Has she given you the rent for the first month?"

"No, but she will. I'm sure she'll be by in the next day or two. I'm looking forward to meeting her. Samantha says she's quite attractive. You might want to stick around. There doesn't seem to be a husband in the picture."

Brett tucked his head slightly and eyed his aunt over his glasses. "That's the last thing I need right now. Besides. What Samantha Evans calls attractive and what I call attractive are probably two entirely different things," Brett said, kissing his aunt on the forehead. "I'll be by again tomorrow. Meanwhile, behave yourself."

"What fun is that?" Ida Carter asked with a twinkle in her eye.

David Norsworthy heard the jingle of the bell on the front door of the art gallery and looked up from his computer. "Brett. What brings you to the coast today? Checking on your aunt or doing an exposé on the politics of the Cove?"

"A little politics and a little personal. Something going on out at Walker's Point Wednesday, but I'll be here the whole week trying to tie up some loose ends at Lonewild. Hey, I hear it's leased to someone you know. Do you think I could get a phone number? I need to make arrangements to clean out the upstairs, but I don't want to barge in on the new renters."

"I can do better than that. Come with me," he said, getting up and walking to the edge of the stairs. "Listen. Since you can't stay at Lonewild now, why don't you stay with Elizabeth and me? It's kind of lonely around the house with Jess away at college. Plenty of room."

"I just checked in at the inn. Paper's paying for it this time. But I'll take a rain check if you don't mind. I'm sure I'll be coming back regularly to check on Aunt Ida."

"Sure thing. Just let us know. Even if Jess is home for the weekend, we still have a guest room with your name on it."

"That's great, man. I appreciate it. How's Nathan?"

David's younger brother Nathan had met his wife Tracy when she spent a month in Wentworth Cove a couple of years ago. He'd easily persuaded her to give up her life in Boston and embrace small-town living, and they were married within six months.

"Gonna be a proud papa in about three months. Tracy's pregnant, and they're all giddy about it. Mom's giddy about it too. Another granddaughter. Didn't think my little bro would ever get married and have kids, but I'm so happy for him. There's hope for you."

"No way. Not me. No time in my schedule for that stuff. The *Trib* keeps me so busy I barely have time to eat and sleep. Had to promise my editor a spectacular piece on this Walker's Point thing to get a few extra days off."

"Come upstairs with me," he said, heading for the gallery's second floor.

"Upstairs?"

"To the deck. The renter you need to meet is a painter and went up there to check out the midday light."

"A painter?"

"Yeah, a watercolorist. We sell her paintings here. She's good. Easy on the eyes too."

"Don't you start on me. Aunt Ida already did. Says Samantha Evans told her. I'm certainly not relying on *her* opinion, and I'm not sure about *you*. You're a little too determined to make sure I join the married brotherhood."

"I'm just saying…but you can see for yourself in a minute. Come on."

"Watercolors, huh?" Brett asked under his breath as he followed his friend up the stairs.

Brett caught himself staring at the woman on the deck. Admittedly, she was pretty…in her early thirties would be his guess. Wavy brown hair with blonde highlights. Deep-set, dark blue eyes…almost enigmatic, he thought, but certainly attractive. He had to hand it to Samantha Evans this time.

"Reagan? This is Ida Carter's nephew, Brett Mason," David said. "Came to the Cove to take care of some of the items still at Lonewild. I'll leave you two to sort things out about how and when. Brett, how about lunch at Down East Diner when you finish? For old times' sake?"

"Sure thing. This shouldn't take long and I'm starving."

"Will you join us, Reagan?" David asked.

Her voice was soft and tentative. "Uh, no. No. Thank you, David. I have a lot to do today. But thanks."

Ambivalent thoughts flashed through Brett's mind when David left them alone on the deck. On one hand, he thought it best to get the things out of the house and be on his way. But—and this thought seemed to be outweighing the other one—he wanted to know what was going on behind those beguiling blue eyes. "I don't think I got your last name."

"Hart."

"Like the—" Brett touched his right hand to his chest.

"Without the *e*."

"Yeah, well…I'm in town for the week, and I need to make arrangements to get those things out of the upstairs at Lonewild."

"We're using only the downstairs. It's plenty of room for us. So there's no rush as far as we're concerned." Meredith hadn't mentioned the mysterious upstairs "treasures" again and Reagan hadn't had time to pursue the topic, but she was curious enough to want to see them before they were removed. And she had an idea her daughter would never forgive her if she let that happen. "Actually, I won't be home until late today. Would tomorrow work for you?"

"I guess so. But the sooner the better. I'll be busy later in the week."

"I take my daughter to school, but I should be home by nine."

"Nine it is. Are you sure you won't join us for lunch?" *What are you doing, Mason? Remember what you told David? You don't need a woman in your life right now—especially one you know absolutely nothing about. And one Samantha said was—what was the word she used? Mysterious? Nope. You do not need a mysterious—or any other type— woman distracting you from work.*

"I'm sure," Reagan answered. But as she turned to walk back into the room, her shoulder brushed his, rendering his self-talk null and void.

"Bet you never thought you'd have something in common with Samantha Evans. You thought she was hot, didn't you? I could tell." David eyed his friend knowingly when they'd placed their order at Down East Diner.

"She's not bad. Not bad at all," Brett admitted, remembering the way she had casually brushed a stray lock of her chestnut-brown hair away from her face. Remembering how it almost covered one of her intense blue eyes. Remembering perfectly formed rose-pink lips. Mentally scolding himself for letting his thoughts head in that direction. "But I'm not in the market. You know I'm married to the *Trib*. There's really no time for anything— or anyone—else in my life right now."

"If not now, when?" David pressed.

"Never would be my guess. Maybe I'm a bit gun shy, David. I don't know. Erica left me scarred. Most people don't know that, but she did."

David had been one of Brett's groomsmen, but truth be told, he was never convinced she was right for his friend. "Wanted to see the world, huh?"

"Yeah, and with someone who could afford to show it to her. Would've been nice to know all that *before* we were married. Kind of obliterated my trust in the opposite sex."

"You were trained as a journalist to be objective, right? Not to stereotype? You can't put all women in the same category as Erica. You know Elizabeth's not like that. Neither is Tracy. Just don't give up. That's all I'm saying."

"I'll take it under advisement," Brett said, but not convincingly.

"There's one more thing, Brett."

"What's that?"

"There's something, well...I don't know how to explain it, but there's something about the deck at the gallery. Something prophetic, maybe?"

"What do you mean something prophetic about the deck?" Brett squinted at his friend.

"Well, two years ago Nathan met Tracy up there, and then about a year after that another couple met there, and they're married now. Not suggesting. Just stating the facts."

"Good thing I'm not superstitious then. Let's eat. I've got a lot to do this afternoon to get ready for Wednesday," Brett said, diving into his burger.

Chapter Five

"Mr. Wilbanks, since everybody already has a partner, could Meredith be in our group for the project?" Daniel Parker asked his history teacher as soon as the new girl had been introduced to the class and groups began working. "I was new last year, and I remember how it was not to know anybody."

"Great idea, Daniel. You and Landon would be a good group for her to join. Thanks for volunteering."

"Sure. No prob." Actually, Daniel's offer wasn't entirely altruistic. He'd heard his mom and dad talking about a new family who'd moved to Wentworth Cove recently from New York...and since the class was studying the thirteen original colonies, and Landon and Daniel had drawn New York for their project...well, maybe she would be a good resource. Besides, she was kind of cute, with long, wavy brown hair and blue-green eyes. A really nice combination, he thought.

Since Daniel had finished his chemotherapy for leukemia a few weeks before school started, his own sandy brown hair had grown back and he was no longer wearing his Red Sox cap to school. He was thankful he didn't have to explain that to Meredith.

"Hi, I'm Daniel and this is Landon. We're doing research on one of the thirteen original colonies, New York, and have to present it to the class in a week."

"I'm from New York," Meredith said.

"Oh, wow. What a coincidence," Landon said and cut his eyes suspiciously toward Daniel. "What are the odds?"

"Do you have a nickname?" Daniel asked, ignoring his friend.

"A nickname?"

"Yeah. Does anyone call you anything other than Meredith?"

"Not really… Well, my mom calls me Mere sometimes. Is that what you mean?"

"Sort of. Has anyone ever called you Merry…like in Merry Christmas?"

"Nope. That's a new one."

"Well, if you don't mind I'm gonna call you Merry."

"Why?"

"Well, Landon gave me a nickname, Tex, when I was new and I liked it. So I'll give you a nickname because you're new."

"Okay," Meredith said with a shrug. "Let's get started on the project. History is my favorite subject so I don't want to waste time."

"It is? Cool. What part of New York colonial life do you want to research?"

Landon looked at Daniel, his eyebrows raised knowingly.

"What?" Daniel asked, feigning innocence.

"You tell *me* what." Landon countered with a grin, giving his friend's upper arm a friendly punch.

Reagan Hart had studied her daughter's face when she entered the front office of Kennebunk Middle School, where she'd told Meredith to wait. Had the first day at this new school met her expectations? Had she made any friends? Did she like her teachers? Did she have any trouble opening her locker? Had she eaten lunch alone?

Usually chatty after school, Meredith hadn't said a word by the time they reached the car, and this time her mother couldn't read her. As they drove away, Reagan broke down and asked. "So...how was your first day?"

"It was okay."

"Just okay? Did you meet any girls you think you might like as well as Maisie and Kelsey?"

"I didn't really meet any girls," Meredith answered. "A couple said hi, but that was about all. I met some boys, though."

"You met boys but no girls? I'm not ready for this." *Seventh grade? I mean, I'm* really *not ready for this.*

"Oh, Mom. They were just friendly. That's all. One was anyway. The others just went along with him. I'm in their history class and the teacher put me in their group for a project. Then they asked me to eat lunch with them, so I did. The friendly one was new last year, so I guess he remembers how it was."

"Well, that was nice of him, huh?"

"Yeah. He lives in Wentworth Cove too."

"I want you to have friends. Just don't go into too much detail with anyone. Remember that our last name's Hart now. You won't slip up, will you?"

"No, Mom. I won't slip up. I like Hart better than Loper anyway. New beginning. New name. Makes sense."

"You've been really cool about this move, sweet girl. I'm so sorry I had to uproot you and move you away from your good friends."

"It's okay. I know you did it for me."

"For both of us, honey," Reagan admitted. She wanted to avoid Jared as much as she wanted to keep Meredith away from him. She hadn't been able to reconcile the Jared who sold drugs to supplement his already six-figure income to the Jared she had met and fallen in love with when she was a freshman in college. She'd had some minor surgery, and Jared was her anesthesiologist. He'd flirted with her before the surgery and stepped up the attention afterwards. He was seven years older and a first-year resident.

The attention was welcome. Her parents had sold their house, packed up everything they owned, and moved to Europe when she and Ryan were both settled in their respective universities. "Dad's job," they'd explained to her and her brother. But Reagan suspected they'd wanted to move for years, and with the twins out of the house, that was the perfect time.

It was just as well, Reagan had often thought. Their parents hadn't played much of a role in their lives anyway. Reagan and Ryan had been raised by a string of nannies who came and went through what seemed to Reagan like a revolving door. Maybe it was inevitable she'd fall victim to the charms of an older guy, marry after dating for only a couple of months, and get pregnant in their first year of marriage. College was put on hold...and was still on hold. Despite that, she'd found her calling when Meredith came along. She felt she was born to be a mother and had put her heart and soul into raising her daughter.

There was nothing she wouldn't do for her. Even if it meant giving up everything she'd ever known and a city in which she'd spent her entire life. But things were different now. And not so bad, she had to admit. She'd thought Wentworth Cove would be a place of refuge for her, and so far she felt safe and welcome in this picturesque New England village. And Lonewild. Everything about the house seemed right for her and her daughter.

"Hey, I just thought of something. I met Miss Carter's nephew today. Apparently he's taking care of moving things out of Lonewild for her. He's coming over in the morning to clean out the upstairs."

"No! He can't do that!"

"What is wrong with you, Mere? It's their stuff. They can move it out if they want to."

"You have to see it first."

"Okay, okay. I'll go up as soon as we get home, but I need to stop by the gallery first. I have a couple of framed prints to drop off. And I want to ask David if he's heard of any part-time jobs I might be interested in."

"Why can't you just work for him? That would be perfect. He knows you worked in an art gallery in New York, right?"

"His gallery's too small. Besides, his wife and mom help him. I need a job that can pay me a decent salary. Part time, of course, so I can still take care of the online business. I think we'll be fine if I can get about twenty hours a week. Just enough to pay the rent. Then the paintings and prints can take care of the rest, and we won't have to dip into savings."

"I want you to have time to paint, Mom. You can't quit painting."

"I don't plan to," Reagan said as she peered through the windshield at the remaining colors of late fall. "You don't think I'd move all the way up here to the beautiful Maine coast and not paint, do you? I'm totally inspired."

The snow that dusted the ground earlier had stopped, and the roads were clear. Reagan was glad. Driving on snow-covered roads was a new skill she wasn't in a hurry to master. She'd always thought of public transportation as a blessing and hadn't minded not having a car in the city.

"And how are our newest Cove residents doing?" David asked as Reagan and Meredith entered the gallery.

"Meredith, I hear you went to school today. How'd that go?"

"It was okay. I met a couple of people...and got a ton of homework."

"Just remember you were the one who wanted to go to school," Reagan reminded her daughter. "I probably would've gone easy on the homework, but you'll never know now, will you?"

"Yeah. All that extra time and nothing to do. Nowhere to go. No one to go with. I guess I'll take the homework along with the friends."

"Your choice. Then no complaining about homework, huh?"

"I can't make that promise, Mom. David, would you mind if I go upstairs and start on it while you and Mom talk?"

"Sure. There's a desk by the closet and a table on the deck. Take your pick."

"Thanks."

Reagan's eyes scanned the room as Meredith bounded up the stairs. Oh, how she wished David needed part time help in the gallery. She already missed her job in New York. Missed being surrounded by the work of talented artists. Missed meeting the people who stopped in— sometimes just to browse.

"I was wondering if you'd heard from any of those galleries in Kennebunkport." She turned to David. "I'd like to find something as soon as possible. I guess as much to pass the time now that Meredith's in school as to make some money. Don't get me wrong. The money will certainly come in handy."

"I've heard back from two of them, but neither one needs help at this time. I did hear about something else, though. Don't know if you'd be interested."

"Try me."

"Bernard's Books and Collectibles—it's across the street and a couple of stores down—"

"I went there one time a couple of years ago when I brought you some paintings. I remember an older guy and a younger woman—"

"Bernard has retired completely now and left the shop basically to his assistant, who's been working for him for several years. I heard she's looking for someone to take over for her a few hours a day…especially during the lunch hours and on Saturday. How would you feel about selling books instead of paintings?"

Not as good as selling paintings, Reagan thought. *But beggars can't be choosers, and maybe it can be temporary until I find something else.*

"It's a charming shop," she said. "And I kind of like the idea of working this close to the house if I'm going to have to work weekends when Meredith's not in school. I'm still a little iffy about leaving her alone." A lot iffy, if Reagan was being honest with herself.

"The good thing is that you could probably take her with you. If not, she could always come over here. You wouldn't have to leave her alone if you were uncomfortable with it. Why don't you go across the street now while Meredith is happily—and I use that term loosely—working on homework upstairs?"

"Thanks, David. I'm going to owe you and Elizabeth a thousand and one favors for everything you've done for us."

Yes, Reagan remembered this shop, and it all came rushing back to her when she recognized that unmistakable and enchanting smell that only old books can emit—the combined aroma of worn leather bindings and yellowing pages. It had been two or three years, but she thought she also remembered the young lady who greeted her. *Maddie? Maggie?*

"Welcome to Bernard's. Something I can help you find?"

"I'm Reagan Hart. David told me you—"

The woman stepped from behind the counter and stuck out her hand. "Am I glad to see you! I'm Maggie Culwell. I was hoping you'd be interested. I can really use the help. How would you feel about twenty-five hours a week to start out? We can probably increase it if you want to. That is, if this traffic keeps up. It seems there's renewed interest in used and first edition books. Who knew? I thought most people were reading ebooks these days."

Maggie, that's right. Lovely in a natural sort of way. Tall and thin with dark brown hair pulled back in a ponytail. No makeup that Reagan could tell, but some women didn't seem to need it and Maggie was one of them.

"I guess they're like me. I like to turn pages—real ones—made of paper," Reagan said.

"Guess so. Anyway, I could use some help if you're interested. Say ten to two weekdays and twelve to five on Saturday? We're closed on Sunday."

"Actually, those hours are perfect."

"Good. Have you ever worked in a bookstore?"

"No, but I've worked part time for several years in an art gallery. I guess selling is selling, but I know I'll have to familiarize myself with the inventory. Could I shadow you for a day or two?"

"Of course. Would you like to start tomorrow?"

Tomorrow. I didn't expect to have to— "Well, I guess I could. Wait—I have a couple of meetings tomorrow. Could I start Wednesday maybe?"

"Sure. We open at ten. Want to be here then?"

"Ten o'clock sharp. And thank you for the opportunity."

"Thank *you*. I was getting desperate."

As Reagan walked back across the street to the gallery, she thought once again about how much had transpired in such a short time—the perfect house with a natural privacy fence of stately pines, a school for Meredith with an understanding staff, and now a part-time job with just enough hours to allow her to take Meredith to school and pick her up every day. But was three hundred miles enough distance from her ex-husband? That was the question that sometimes kept her awake at night. Sometimes invaded her thoughts during the day. Sometimes took away her appetite or made her crave comfort food.

The main question that plagued her was whether she had overlooked something. She'd legally changed her and her daughter's last name, left no forwarding address, told no one but Ryan where she was moving...even though it had been hard to leave Henry—who'd been a father figure to her and a doting grandfather to Meredith—and some special friends. She thought about her website but couldn't figure out any way Jared could track her down by that because the only way to contact her was through the website itself. No physical address. No email address. No phone number. No new last name on the site. But she still wondered if she had dotted all her *i*'s and crossed all her *t*'s.

Chapter Six

"Mom, when are you going upstairs to look at those things before they're taken away?" Meredith asked as soon as she had taken off her coat and kicked off her shoes in the front entry. She was nothing if not persistent.

"Let's go now. Then I can start dinner without you hounding me."

"You're gonna be glad I hounded you, and you're gonna be glad you saw them before that guy comes to take them away."

As Reagan followed her daughter up the stairs and stopped on the landing, her breath caught in her throat. Light spilled from the west-facing window whose curtains had been drawn back, probably by Meredith, to give her a better look at the paintings that sat on the floor and on chairs in front of her.

"So? What do you think?" Meredith asked with an expectancy in her voice.

"Oh, wow. These are amazing."

"Yeah. That's what I thought. They remind me of yours. Not as good, of course. But good, don't you think? What do you think he'll do with them?"

"Well, I know what he *should* do with them," Reagan said, examining them more closely.

"What?"

"Either take them to David or let me sell them for him on my website."

"Good idea. You think they're good enough, don't you? I thought you would."

"They're beautiful. I wonder if she's ever sold any. Got your phone in your pocket?"

"Yeah. Want me to Google her name?"

"Do it. These are all signed 'Ida Carter.' If she's sold any on the internet, there should be evidence. If not, I wonder if David knows about them. I don't remember ever seeing any Ida Carter paintings in his gallery, though. I know he'd be happy to have some of these."

"I can't find anything linking Ida Carter with paintings," Meredith reported after searching her name. "There's an article in the local paper about a birthday party a couple of years ago when she turned eighty-five."

"I never thought I'd live in a place where the newspaper had a write-up about someone's birthday. That's kind of cute when you think about it, though. A far cry from New York City, but that's what we wanted."

Tuesday had dawned bright and crisp with the assurance of a beautiful fall day. The snow that had fallen intermittently on Monday had finally melted and left in its absence a winter blue sky devoid of clouds and a promise of sunshine for at least part of the day.

Reagan heard the crunch of gravel in the driveway as Brett pulled up promptly at nine o'clock…shortly after she returned from taking Meredith to school. She looked out the kitchen window out of caution. Would she ever feel completely at ease again?

"You're prompt, Mr. Mason," Reagan said, opening the kitchen door.

"I have a lot to do today. You won't mind if I start loading up things in my car? I'm sure you'd like me to get out of your way as soon as possible too."

"About that—"

"About what?"

"I went upstairs to see how much was left...to get an idea of how much time it would take to remove it, of course..."

Reagan wanted to tread softly here. Didn't want Brett to think she and Meredith had been snooping since they were supposed to use only the downstairs, but she also wanted him to know these weren't just some paintings of an inexperienced amateur. "And, well...I was blown away by the beauty of the paintings. Did your aunt do all of them?"

"She did. She took up painting about four years ago. Then about two years ago, she started losing her eyesight. Macular degeneration. It was pretty sad because she loved painting so much, but she never let her circumstances get her down. You haven't met her, have you?"

"No, but I will this afternoon. I'm taking her the rent check. That is, unless I can give it to you. Losing her eyesight? That's too bad. Really. Such a talent, and now she can't paint at all?"

"No. Aunt Ida gave up painting a few months ago. You'd better take the check to her if you don't mind. She wouldn't give up a chance to meet you. She'll want you to bring it to her every month. That won't be a problem, will it? I'll warn you, though. She might want to talk about Lonewild. She lived here almost all of her adult life. When you think about it, it's amazing she could leave it as easily as she did."

"I look forward to meeting her."

"I'd better get up there and start cleaning out. I don't want to take up your whole morning," Brett said, heading toward the stairs.

"Before you start...could we...could I propose something? I don't mean to be nosy, but I was wondering what you're planning to do with the paintings."

"I'm really not sure. Just going to pack them away for now. Probably take them back to my apartment. Aunt Ida doesn't want them. But I don't have the heart to get rid of them."

"She doesn't?"

"She didn't even want any to hang on the walls of her new apartment at Sundown."

"I have a proposition," Reagan said.

"Sounds intriguing. I have a busy day ahead of me...but I might be persuaded to come back tomorrow." Brett winked, and Reagan could feel the color rising from her neck to her cheeks. "Sorry. You were saying..."

Reagan regrouped. "I was wondering if you—if she— would let me sell them for her. I'm a watercolorist, too, and I have a website. There's a market for these. By the way, has David seen them?"

"I suggested that a couple of years back, but she wouldn't have it. I'm afraid she thinks they're not good enough."

"Oh, but they are. I worked in an art gallery for several years. Take it from me. These are exceptional."

"Maybe you can persuade her of that. Good luck, though. I've tried. But the fact that you're an artist too... That might have some bearing on her valuing your opinion over mine. She thinks I'm just flattering her. Meanwhile, I'll get them out of your way, and if you need them back you can contact me. Here's my card."

"Thank you. I'll talk with her this afternoon and let you know either way. Can I help you pack them up?"

"I won't turn down that offer. Let me get the boxes out of my car."

45

"Oh, I have plenty of empty boxes and would love to get rid of them."

Working in tandem, Reagan and Brett had the upstairs cleared in less than an hour. As she helped him gather the paintings, she was amazed again at the talent of her landlady. She was pretty sure that even the gallery in the city where she had worked would be interested in these. But she'd try them on her website first. Test the water and see if the public felt the way she did about them.

This was the first sunny day since Reagan's arrival in Wentworth Cove, and the brisk fall air brought a yearning for adventure. Reagan relished the thought of doing a little exploring before beginning her new job at Bernard's Books and Collectibles on Wednesday. Since it hadn't taken long to rid the upstairs of the few things that were left from Ida Carter's move to Sundown Assisted Living Center in Kennebunk, there was plenty of time for new discoveries in the area. Miss Carter would be the first stop on her adventure. She had a rent check to deliver and an artist she hoped to persuade to go public with her watercolors.

Maybe it was because the weather had been overcast since Saturday. Maybe it was because she'd been too busy to notice. But the last red and orange leaves that were hanging onto the maples and oaks for dear life inspired Reagan to unpack her paints and brushes as soon as possible. She'd painted Wentworth Cove mostly in the summer, but it was resplendent in the fall...a realization that made her even happier she had decided to uproot Meredith and move to this charming village.

Pulling her car into one of the few empty spaces in the parking lot at Sundown, Reagan thought about what she could say to change Miss Carter's mind about selling her paintings. Not being able to settle on anything that sounded exactly right, she decided to play it by ear. Get a feel for her personality first. What was the word Samantha had used to describe Reagan's new landlady? Unusual?

Reagan was a bit surprised when she walked in. She didn't know exactly what to expect, but not this. This place looked more like her parents' country club than how she had pictured an assisted living facility in her mind. She made her way to the information desk, told the silver-haired receptionist who she was and that she had come to see Ida Carter.

"You and everybody else in the area," the lady said, smiling. "You passed her on your way in. She's the one in the yellow pantsuit sitting right by the door. She's our unofficial official greeter. I'm surprised she didn't say something to you when you entered."

"Thank you. I won't be here long."

"Stay as long as you want. She loves visitors. In fact, you might find it difficult to get away. Miss Carter has a way about her that just draws people in and beckons them to stay. Well, you'll see for yourself. You'd better grab that folding chair by the wall. She's going to want you to sit close."

Strange, Reagan thought, but didn't her nephew say she was losing her eyesight?

She walked over and stood right in front of her new landlady. "Miss Carter? I'm Reagan Hart. I'm leasing Lonewild and I brought the first month's check."

"Sit down, young lady. Let me get a better look at you. Pardon if I get in your personal space, but I don't see so well these days." Reagan sat down and pulled her chair closer. Ida leaned in to get a better look. "You're a pretty thing. What did you say your name is?"

"Reagan. Reagan Hart."

"Reagan. That's an unusual first name. I know of only one other...oh, never mind. How do you like my Lonewild?"

"My daughter and I—"

"That's right. You have a daughter. How old is she?"

"She's twelve—going on twenty. The joy of my life."

"Her name?"

The woman was nosy, but somehow Reagan didn't mind. Ida Carter had an air of trustworthiness that made you willing to open yourself up to her. "Meredith."

"And how do you and Meredith like my little cottage on the coast? Is it roomy enough for you? When my nephew gets the stuff out of the upstairs, you can spread out. I don't want you thinking you have to use just the downstairs. I know that's what the contract said, but that was just until we could clear it out. I would like the whole house to be lived in and cared for."

"He came this morning and took care of it."

"Good for him. Now you consider the whole house yours to love and enjoy. A little lagniappe for you and your daughter," Ida Carter said with a big smile.

"We'll do that. I'm sure Meredith would like to think of the upstairs as her domain. That way I can turn the second downstairs bedroom into a studio for me." Having a room to set up her easels and watercolors downstairs would be a dream come true for Reagan. Could this move get any better? A part-time job. A studio. A safe place away from Jared.

"What kind of work do you do?" Ida asked.

Reagan eyed her new friend and wondered what type of response her answer would elicit. "I'm a painter, Miss Carter. A watercolorist, actually."

"You're a… Wait a minute. What did you say your last name is? Hart?"

"That's my name now, but I paint under the name of Reagan Loper. I was married—actually newly divorced—when I started painting."

"That's impossible. That's too much of a coincidence. *You're* Reagan Loper? *The* Reagan Loper who has paintings in Norsworthy Art Gallery?"

"You've seen my work then?"

"Seen your work? You're my inspiration, young lady. What are the odds Reagan Loper would lease my beloved Lonewild? It brings tears to my old, worn-out eyes. Miss Loper...Miss Hart...Reagan...you're the reason the last four years have been the best years of my life."

"What do you mean?"

"I used to go to David's gallery for the sheer beauty of the paintings. Never bought anything. Much to David's dismay, I imagine," Ida said, laughing. "I would go by there about once a week, when I was still able to drive, and stare at the beautiful artwork in his shop. Yours were always my favorites. Then one day I said to myself, 'Ida, maybe you could do something like that. You'll never know if you don't try.' So I contacted an art teacher in Kennebunkport who gives private lessons. It took me a while to get the hang of it—I'm not sure I really ever got the hang of it—but I was satisfied enough with my work that I could pretend to myself I was good. Anyway, it was therapeutic and I enjoyed seeing the world with new eyes. Every time I saw what I considered a thing of beauty, I would think about painting it. You have no idea what a difference that made in my life." She patted Reagan's hand.

"I might have an idea. Believe it or not, my story isn't that different from yours."

"The irony is that a couple of years after I began noticing the beauty all around me, my sight started failing. Then I got the devastating news that I could lose the use of my eyes completely. Can you imagine? You start to see things for the first time...and then you can't see anything at all. I still have some sight remaining, but it's getting worse and my doctor says there's nothing he can do about it."

"I'm so sorry, Miss Carter."

"Oh, honey. Don't feel sorry for me. I've had a good life. I still do. I have so many friends who come to see me. I'm content. One part of my life is over, but that doesn't mean I have to curl up and die, now does it?"

"Of course not," Reagan said, amazed at the woman's attitude. "I'm sure it was hard on you having to leave your home, but I want to assure you that my daughter and I will take good care of it. I brought your rent check, and I'll bring it every month. It will be good to see you again."

"Maybe you could bring your daughter next time. I never had any children of my own, but I've always enjoyed young people. I love my nephew like a son, helped raise him after his parents died and he moved in with his grandparents, but he lives in Augusta, so I don't get to see him as often as I'd like."

"I talked with him about the watercolors this morning. They *are* good, Miss Carter. I would like the opportunity to sell them for you...that is, if you're interested. I don't want to meddle in your business, but I think people should have the benefit of knowing what a good artist you are."

Ida Carter sat up a little straighter in her chair. "You think so? You really think anyone would buy them? I value your opinion, but I find that hard to believe."

"I do. I also think we should show them to David. I think he'll agree with me and want to put some in the gallery."

"Oh, I don't think so. Brett has been after me to do that, but I know they're not that good. I'd be embarrassed to show them to him, considering the quality of art he sells."

"Then let me do it. I know David. He won't tell me he likes them if he doesn't. But either way, I know I could sell them on my website. Think of it this way... Why should you be so selfish as to deny people the beauty of Ida Carter's watercolors?" Smiling, Reagan leaned over and squeezed Ida's hand.

"I think Brett was going to throw them away. I imagine he has by now."

"I asked him not to," Reagan assured her. "He was going to take them to his house until I had a chance to talk with you. He thinks they're good too. So far that's two against one…make that three against one. Meredith thinks they're great. She actually saw them before I did."

"I'll give it some thought. That's as far as I can go right now. You have to understand that I started painting just for me. I never intended to show them to anyone."

"And I don't mean to invade your privacy. Just let me know what you decide, but I hope you won't deny people the beauty of your work. Think about the inspiration you got from my paintings. You might be able to do the same for someone."

"I'll think about it. You've given me a new perspective. I never dreamed I would meet the person who inspired me to pick up a brush. What are the odds?"

"It's been a pleasure to meet and chat with you, but I'd better go. I'll see you next month with the November check. You can let Mr. Mason know if you decide to let me sell some paintings."

"You can come back sooner if you'd like and bring your daughter."

"I'm sure she'd like that. She loves everything about Lonewild, and I know she'd like to meet the owner."

On her way out of the facility, Reagan wondered if she'd made any headway in persuading her landlady to let her sell the watercolors, but one thing she did know: If Miss Ida Carter was truly known as the matriarch of Wentworth Cove, it wasn't a misnomer.

Maggie Culwell was unlocking the front door of Bernard's Books and Collectibles on Wednesday morning when Reagan walked up. "I thought it would be better if I didn't park right in front of the store, so I'm in David's parking lot. Is there a better place? I hate to take up one of his spaces, but I didn't want to take up a space in front of the bookstore."

"I should have told you. There are two spots behind the store. Why don't you bring your car around. I'll unlock the back door for you. And remind me to give you a key."

"Be right there."

Reagan wasn't sure why she was looking forward to this morning so much. Maybe it was because Maggie had seemed warm and friendly on Monday. Most of her friends had slowly drifted away when Jared went to prison. They stayed with her during the trial, but they were married, and she no longer fit in as a single woman. It was just as well, she thought. She needed to concentrate on Meredith and her job at the gallery.

While she was married, she'd spent her spare time making a home for her husband and daughter... decorating, cooking, and taking care of everybody's schedules. She divorced Jared as soon as the trial was over and decided she needed something else to fill her hours— to keep her mind occupied. So she decided to try her hand at painting. After taking lessons for about six months, she settled on watercolor as her medium of choice. The painting had partially filled a void in her life, but she'd missed companionship.

"Perfect," Maggie said, opening the back door to let her in and handing her a key. "Now we're out of the way and no one will ding our car doors. I might be a little obsessive about mine, but it's my first new car and I plan to keep it for a very long time."

"Yeah, I understand. I bought mine a couple of weeks before we left the city. For the last few years, I haven't owned a car. I always rented one when we'd drive to Boston to see my brother."

"You have a brother? Nice. I always wanted a brother. I have a sister, Annie. You'll probably meet her soon. We're close, but it would be nice to have a brother."

"We're actually twins, and I'm sure you'll meet him soon too. He lives in Boston but checks in on us about once a month. And he's happy we're so much closer now.

He can drive up any weekend." Ryan had remained a bachelor, and Reagan had never tried to set him up with any of her friends, but an idea was forming in the back of her mind. She'd have to get to know Maggie a little better, but looking at her now, Reagan thought she just might check all of Ryan's boxes. He tended to be more interested in natural beauty and women who wore little or no makeup. Check!

"I look forward to meeting him. Are you ready to start learning the ropes? Let me show you a few things while we don't have any customers."

The morning passed so quickly that Reagan was surprised when Maggie asked her if she felt like staying alone for an hour while she went home for lunch.

"I'm fine with that as long as I can call if something I don't know how to handle comes up."

"Of course. Can I bring you something when I come back?"

"I discovered Carson's Market Monday, so I'm good."

Thoughtful. Check!

Brett Mason sat in his car in front of Bernard's Books and Collectibles, chastising himself for not being at work on the article he needed to have to his editor by five o'clock. Just a short conversation with Reagan Hart, he rationalized, and he'd go back to the inn and get started on it. It shouldn't take much more than an hour, two at the most, to write. He'd taken good notes.

On the passenger seat next to him lay five of his aunt's best watercolors. At least, to his way of thinking they were her best. But what did he know? He'd get the opinion of an expert. And it was just his luck that an expert lived right here in Wentworth Cove. He'd be silly not to consult her, wouldn't he?

He gathered the paintings, walked to the door...and stopped. *Why are you really here, Mason? Is it that innate desire you seem to have to keep your life in a turmoil?* He put his hand on the doorknob but hesitated again. *Fish or cut bait, buddy.* He turned the knob and walked in.

Chapter Seven

Brett Mason was the last person Reagan expected to see on her first day at work. The bookstore had been quiet since Maggie left for lunch, and she would just as soon it stayed that way. As comfortable as she felt being alone with customers at the art gallery, she wasn't quite as sure of herself when it came to selling books.

Her mind seemed to entertain a thousand thoughts all at once. What was he doing here? Had something happened to his aunt? Were they changing their minds about wanting to rent Lonewild? *Please, God, don't let it be that. I can't uproot Meredith again.*

But she and Ida had both signed a contract, and Ida seemed to like her, so it couldn't be that. She noticed he was carrying something tucked under his arm. She also noticed *him*. For the first time, actually. When they'd met at the gallery and when he'd come to Lonewild to clean out the upstairs, she hadn't given him a second thought, a second glance...but now. She wouldn't consider him exactly handsome...a little nerdy, in fact, with his black-framed glasses and short-cropped hair. But his shoulders were broader than she remembered. His dark brown eyes seemed to smile before the rest of his face did. And he looked pretty snappy in a navy wool shirt and neatly pressed brown slacks.

She decided to keep it light. "Can I interest you in a rare first edition? I have a *Great Gatsby* here for a mere $2,500…and I hear that's quite a bargain."

"I would consider that, but I already have three or four of those pesky Fitzgerald first editions lying around the house gathering dust. Got anything a little less common? Say, a signed *Frankenstein*?"

"We don't have one in the store, but if you'd like, I'd be happy to try to find one for you online."

"How long have you been working here? A couple of hours? Maggie's taught you well," Brett said with a twinkle in his eye and a lopsided grin.

"What makes you think she had to teach me? I guess it never occurred to you that I could have an innate sense of customer service."

"Ouch. The lady can sell books *and* put a guy in his rightful place."

"You're actually my first customer. Let's start over. Can I help you find something, sir?"

"I hear you met Aunt Ida."

"I did. She's delightful."

"She was quite taken with you too. Couldn't believe you're the one who's leasing Lonewild. Seems your watercolors inspired her to start painting. That's quite a coincidence."

"It was a humbling experience for me. I'd never considered anyone would like my paintings that much and actually get inspiration from them."

"Well, she did, and she was unbelievably excited to meet you."

"Is there something I can do for you? Is she okay?" Reagan hoped her uneasiness wasn't evident.

"She's fit as a fiddle. Well, with the exception of her eyes. You know she's losing her eyesight, right?"

"Yes, but her attitude is amazing. She just kind of blew it off like it's no big deal. That would freak me out, I think. Of all the senses, sight is probably the most important to me."

"Yeah. I can't decide if she hides her true feelings or if she really is able to make lemonade out of lemons. I tend to think it's the latter."

"An admirable trait."

"Indeed."

"So…" Reagan wasn't necessarily eager to end this exchange, but she *was* curious about why Brett had dropped by.

"I guess you're wondering why I'm here."

"Well, a little. If you don't want that *Frankenstein*. It *would* be a great investment."

"Investments like that cost money, so I'd better pass on it today."

"I'm afraid books are all we have here."

"I came for advice."

"Advice? From me? Or did you come to see Maggie? She's at lunch, but she should be back around one-ish."

"No. I came to see you." He laid the paintings on the counter. "I need to do something with these and I was thinking maybe you could…" He hesitated, not sure exactly what he was thinking she could do.

"Could what? I'd be happy to help you sell them if that's what Miss Carter wants. When I talked to her yesterday, she said she'd think about it. Has she already decided?"

"She decided to leave it up to me. I think they're good, but I wanted your honest opinion. Would they sell? She doesn't think so, but I can't bear to think about getting rid of them without trying. Of course, I don't have the slightest idea where to start. She doesn't want me to talk to David."

"She told me the same thing, but I know David's taste and I know he would think they're good. There is another option, though."

"What's that?" Brett asked.

"I sell some of my paintings on my website, and I'd be happy to put them on there. See if we get any bites."

"That's a thought. You wouldn't mind?"

"No. I'd like to. It would be such a waste to let them rot in an attic or basement. Art is to be enjoyed." Just then the door opened again and two young women walked in. "I'm sorry. I need to—"

"Of course."

"Wish me luck."

As was his journalist's nature, Brett observed Reagan interacting with the customers. They asked about a specific book, and she went to a database to check on its availability. He heard her say, "I'll be happy to order that for you," and they apparently declined her offer and left.

"Whew," she said, walking back to where Brett was standing. "I really wasn't ready to answer a lot of questions."

"You were very professional," Brett said, giving her a thumbs-up. "I'll bet they thought you were the owner of the shop."

"And I'm pretty sure they could tell this was my first day."

"Would you like to discuss the paintings over lunch? When Maggie gets back? She does give you a lunch break, doesn't she?"

"I brought a sandwich, but I'm working through lunch so I can leave at two and pick up my daughter from school."

"Dinner then? It would have to be a late one. I have an article to get to my editor before five, but I'd like to know if you think these are appropriate to start with." It was as good an excuse as any, and Brett was rather proud of himself for thinking of it.

"I don't know. I don't really want to leave my daughter alone at Lonewild since we just moved here."

"Bring her. Or would she be too bored?"

"Probably not, but she might have quite a bit of homework. She mentioned a history project that's taking a lot of her time. Tomorrow maybe? I'll ask Elizabeth if she can pick up Meredith and bring her to the gallery after school. I get off at two. Is that too late for lunch?"

"Not at all. Better for me, too, really. Two it is. Meet here and walk to Down East Diner or Lobster Bistro? Not much of a choice here."

"Either one is fine with me. Both are better than a turkey sandwich, which is what I'm having today."

"I brought what I think are the five best paintings. Do you have time to take a quick look and tell me if you think they're the best?"

"Sure. Let's see what you brought. Then we can talk in more detail tomorrow about how to best present them to the public," Reagan said as Brett laid them out on the counter.

In high school Brett Mason had suffered unrequited crushes, agonized over dance invitation rejections, and borne the anguish of overhearing a group of cheerleaders calling him a nerd. Hiding hurt and disappointment had become second nature to him. In college, though, things were different. Nerds seemed to be in demand for study groups, and that's where he'd met Erica. Eventually, the group morphed from six members to only the two of them, and study sessions turned into kissing sessions. When he finally worked up the nerve to ask her to marry him, he was a little surprised she said yes. Rejection had been more or less expected by then.

A couple of years into the marriage Brett realized she had expected him to graduate and earn a six-figure salary.

But Brett wanted only to write, so he took a position with the *Augusta Tribune* and worked his way up to their chief political reporter. The pay, however, wasn't what Erica had expected him to make, so she ran off with the owner of a chain of sporting goods stores, and they moved in together before the divorce was final.

Brett had been on a couple of dates since then, but his heart wasn't in it. A friend had set them up. Otherwise, he wouldn't have gone. But he had no interest in getting hurt again. Once was more than enough.

So why had he come to Bernard's Books and Collectibles fifteen minutes early on Thursday? What was it that kept piquing his interest in his aunt's mysterious tenant? Reagan had said she wouldn't be able to leave for lunch until two o'clock, and here he was, pushing through the door at a quarter till.

He and Maggie had known each other in school. She was a couple of years his junior, but he'd always thought of her as…well, maybe not a friend, but a friendly acquaintance. That he had come early to have a chance to talk to Maggie would be as good an excuse as any other for his early arrival.

"Hi, Brett. You haven't been in here in quite a while. It's good to see you." He'd always thought Maggie mildly attractive. She had a natural kind of beauty, and in the fifteen or so years since they'd graduated from high school she hadn't changed all that much. Today, though, she looked particularly pretty with her dark brown hair falling down her back. And that red dress didn't hurt a bit. Had he been gone *that* long? The years had been good to her, he concluded. He was sure that if she had moved away from Wentworth Cove, she'd be married by now.

"Maggie. You look…wonderful. How've you been?"

"Really good. You?"

"Oh, you know. Same old workaholic Brett."

"Have you come early to steal my helper? She said she was meeting you at two for a late lunch."

"Uh, no. I actually came a little early to see you. How long has it been? A couple of years?"

"At least."

"I should come by more often. Maybe I will now. We should catch up."

"Sure. That would be great. I'll get Reagan. She's in the office. I don't mind if she leaves now. We're not busy…as you can see."

"I'm here, Maggie. Hello, Brett," Reagan said as she stepped out from behind a knotty-pine bookshelf. "I wasn't eavesdropping. Just coming to tell Maggie the inventory is finished. Let me grab my purse and coat."

After overhearing their exchange, Reagan wondered if maybe Brett was interested in Maggie and was using the advice on the watercolors to have a reason to come to the bookstore. Oh well. What did it matter? She certainly wasn't interested in developing any type of personal relationship with him. The guy was only taking care of Lonewild for his aunt and allowing Reagan to sell her paintings. Period. Full stop.

"What would you like for lunch?" Brett asked, helping her on with her coat. "My treat since you're giving me free advice. The advice is free, isn't it? Or is that being presumptuous?"

"I've always heard you get what you pay for, so I might need to order surf and turf if you want some really good advice."

"Note to self: The lady has some great one-line zingers. Tread softly, Mason," Brett said with a slight wink.

"Actually, I'm happy to be able to help with the paintings. That is my wheelhouse, after all."

"Lobster Bistro is about two blocks down Main Street and around the corner. My car is parked across the street at the gallery. Would you like to ride or walk?"

"Let's walk if you don't mind. I'm already inspired by the lingering of fall colors here on the coast. I thought this would all be gone by now and we'd be covered in a couple of inches of snow for the rest of fall and throughout winter."

"Are you not from the area? We don't usually get that much snow here on the coast. Not as much as the rest of Maine anyway. I live in Augusta, and I'll guarantee we get double what the Cove gets each winter. I don't think David mentioned where you moved from."

"New York City. I've been coming to Wentworth Cove once or twice a year for the last four years, though, so I'm pretty familiar with the area. In the summer mostly. When I bring David some new watercolors, I stay for a couple of days and try to get in some painting. The flowers here are pretty awe-inspiring. Not something we have in the city. Obviously."

"Why did you leave a bustling city and move to our little village?"

"Um…" Reagan wasn't ready to tell her life story to Brett Mason, but she didn't want to be rude. So she hesitated.

Sensing her discomfort, he said, "Forget I asked. Reporter's curse—thinking I'm interviewing everybody I talk to."

"No problem." Reagan understood people's curiosity. What *would* make someone pick up and move to a place that was completely opposite of where she had lived all her life? If she were on the other side of this situation, she would be curious too.

Brett abruptly changed the subject. "I'll have to check out your paintings when I pick up my car this afternoon. I usually just visit with David when I'm in the gallery. Don't think much about looking at what's on the walls and easels."

"I noticed on your business card that you're with the *Augusta Tribune*. Isn't Augusta the capital?"

"Good for you! Most people think the capital of Maine is either Portland or Bangor."

"My eighth grade history teacher drilled those capitals into our heads. I don't think I could forget them if I tried."

"Vermont?" Brett challenged.

"Montpelier."

"Wyoming?"

"Cheyenne."

"Kansas?"

"Topeka."

"You just earned a big piece of apple pie with that surf and turf. The lady not only has some great one-liners, but she also knows her state capitals. Very impressive." Brett was beginning to think his initial impression of Reagan was wrong. This lady seemed more sincere than mysterious…and sharp to boot.

Reagan and Brett arrived at Lobster Bistro, and a waitress seated them in a booth by the window. "Before I forget," Reagan said, "I wanted to tell you that your aunt said we can occupy the upstairs now that you've cleared it, so I plan to move my daughter's bedroom up there and turn that second downstairs bedroom into a studio. The morning light in that room makes it perfect for painting. I thought maybe I'd better run it by you too, though, since you're taking care of the house for her."

"Sure. If that's what Aunt Ida wants. It's totally up to her."

"I haven't told Meredith yet, but she's going to be so excited. She wanted that from day one."

"You're not going to try to move the furniture yourself, are you?"

"I hadn't thought that far yet. So much going on— moving to a new state, getting a new job, enrolling Mere in a new school. It kind of hit all at once. I'm sure it will work itself out, though. I could probably find someone from a moving company who wouldn't mind making a few extra dollars on his day off."

"Bet I could talk David into helping me with that. We could get it done in under an hour."

"So then I would owe *you* surf and turf, right?"

"You catch on fast. Let's order, and then we can talk about how to sell the paintings. When I pick up my car, I'll run in and see if David can help with the furniture before I have to go back to Augusta on Sunday. What day would be convenient for you?"

"I'm not going to be picky when free help is offered, but the sooner the better. Meredith and I will both enjoy being able to spread out."

During the course of the lunch, it was decided that Reagan would list the five watercolors Brett had picked out and see it they got any hits. If any of them caught the public's interest, she suggested they might have some prints made and sell those too. Brett was happy with that plan and said he would bring them when he and David came to move furniture.

"If David hesitates at all—" Reagan started.

"He won't," Brett assured her.

"He and Elizabeth have already done so much for us."

"Then one more little thing won't be a problem. I'm thinking Sunday afternoon might be good because Elizabeth will be able to watch the gallery then. Or if a weekday works better, I think Kate—that's his mom—helps out when he needs her. Have you met her?"

"No."

"You probably will soon. Wentworth Cove is a small town and just about everyone knows just about everyone else. Very different from New York City, huh?"

"Very."

Reagan and Brett continued their conversation over lobster rolls, deciding exactly when Reagan would add Ida's paintings to her website and what price she would put on them. At times they sat and ate without talking. Brett finished his meal first, then leaned back and eyed Reagan. She was proving quite different from what he expected when he first heard a mysterious woman with a child was leasing Lonewild. Nothing like Erica, from what he could tell, but he admonished himself to remain cautious. The last thing he needed was to fully trust someone and have that rug pulled out from under him. He'd married a woman he thought he knew only to find out she was someone else entirely, and he didn't completely trust his judgment anymore.

Chapter Eight

"Hey, Tex!" Landon called across the packed school lunchroom. "You and Merry want to join us?"

"That okay?" Daniel Parker asked his new friend. He had taken the girl under wing and was making sure her transition from New York City to Wentworth Cove was as easy as his had been last year when he moved with his family from Dallas.

"Yeah, okay. My mom says I need to meet some girls, though. Maybe I should—" Meredith started.

"Hey, no problem," Daniel assured her. "We hang out sometimes with a couple of girls named Molly and Isabella. I'll introduce you. You might have a class with one of them."

"I wouldn't know. It'll take time to learn everyone's name."

"Be there in a minute, Landon," Daniel called back. "Let me go find Molly and Isabella. Merry's coming on over."

Meredith was more than okay hanging out with Daniel and Landon and their friend Michael, but her mom wanted her to make some girl friends, so she really should at least try. Who knows, she thought, they might make her miss Maisie and Kelsey less. Anyway, this was where she was destined to be for a while so she might as well settle in.

In a couple of minutes, Daniel came back to the table with two girls in tow. One had straight, long blond hair and was about Meredith's size. The other one was shorter with shoulder-length curly brown hair that looked as though its owner had just washed it and left it to its own devices. The blonde, Daniel explained, was Isabella, and the other one was Molly. They couldn't have looked more unalike, and Meredith wondered if their personalities were that different too.

"Hey, we have language arts together," Molly exclaimed. "You probably don't remember me because everybody's new to you, right?"

"Well, I—"

"That's okay. I know it will take time to get to know everybody. Izzy, do you have any classes with Meredith?" Molly asked her friend.

"You can call her Merry," Daniel cut in. "That's her nickname now. You know…like Landon started calling me Tex last year."

"Mary? Like Jesus's mother?" Molly asked.

"No. Like Merry Christmas." Daniel seemed to feel as though he owned it, so he was quick to explain it.

Molly looked quizzically at Daniel and then at Meredith. "That all right with you?"

Meredith was beginning to like this talkative girl with the wild, curly hair. And she could understand why Isabella, or Izzy as Molly called her, didn't say much. Molly did all the talking in this duo.

"Sure. It's fine," Meredith answered.

"So, Izzy. Do you have any classes with Merry?" Molly repeated.

"Um. I don't think so," Isabella replied.

Meredith was glad to meet a couple of girls, but she began to feel uneasy wondering if they would start asking about her family. She didn't mind talking about her mom, of course. She was proud of what she had accomplished in the past few years with her painting. But she didn't want to have to explain about her dad to anyone. Guys didn't seem to care. They didn't pry. Didn't ask personal questions. But she was afraid girls would be different, and she hadn't had time to figure out what she was going to say if the question came up.

"Hey, Mom. Is it okay if Meredith comes over tomorrow after school to work on the history project?" Daniel asked, bounding into the kitchen after school.

"Who's Meredith? I thought you and Landon were working on a project for history."

"We are, but Merry's new and Mr. Wilbanks said she could be in our group. She's from New York. How's that for luck, huh? And history's her favorite subject, so—"

"Of course she can come over. I'll pick you both up at the usual spot. Will she have a way to get home? Have you met her parents?"

"I don't think she has a dad, but her mom picks her up every day. She just waits inside the office. She never rides the bus."

"Maybe I'd better call her mom and coordinate. Do you have her home number?"

"No, but I have Merry's cell number. She has a cell phone. Did you hear that, Mom? I said, 'She has—'"

"I heard you, Daniel," Emily said with a smile. Her son was a charmer and since he'd been so sick, she and Andy were tempted to give in to him on many things, but this was one thing they were adamant about. No phone until high school. And then only with boundaries. They felt phones were too much of a distraction for kids these days.

"Can you get her mom's number for me? I'm sure she'll want to get to know us before allowing her daughter to come over after school, but it's fine with me. Is Landon coming too?"

"He's going to put it all together in a slide show when we finish. He'd rather do that, and we'd rather do the research. How great was it that the new girl who moved to town is from New York and loves history? Cool, huh?"

"Totally cool, son. I'll call her mom as soon as you get me the number."

"Here you go," Daniel said, scribbling something down on a sticky note as soon as he had reached Meredith.

Emily dialed and Reagan answered immediately. "Reagan, this is Emily Parker, Daniel's mom. He and Meredith are working on a history project for school and he asked if she could come over to work on it. I know you're new to Wentworth Cove, so I wondered if you'd like to come over with her and have a cup of tea while they work. I understand what it's like to be new here. We moved from Dallas a year and a half ago. I was careful about where I let Daniel go at first, so I understand if you are."

"Definitely. Maybe more than is normal since it's just the two of us. When were you talking about? I have a part-time job now."

"If I remember correctly, Daniel mentioned tomorrow after school. I could pick them both up…or you could, if you would be more comfortable with that."

"I get off at two, so I'll be happy to get them. Daniel can tell me how to get to your house. He's been a good friend to Meredith. She talks about him constantly."

On Friday afternoon Emily was sitting at her piano practicing for Sunday's service and thinking about how she'd felt when she settled in Wentworth Cove a little over a year ago. How Kate Norsworthy had been the first to make her feel welcome on a personal level. Being the new pastor's wife, Emily was immediately accepted by the congregation of Wentworth Cove Community Church, but Kate was the one who had come over with her famous Italian cream cake. It was Kate who told her about the history of the town and many of its more prominent people. It was Kate who introduced her family to Josh Whitehall, a young man who was now her son-in-law. He and her twenty-three-year-old daughter Faith had been married for almost three months, and Emily and Andy loved him like a son.

Now Emily had the opportunity to make someone new feel that same Cove welcome that Kate had extended to her. She'd just taken a fresh batch of oatmeal chocolate chip cookies out of the oven, and one batch was already put away in a basket for Reagan and Meredith to take home with them.

Daniel burst through the front door. "Mom! I'm home. Merry and her mom are here too."

"Where are they?" Emily asked. "Did you leave them in the car?"

"Yeah, but they're getting the project stuff. I'll go back and help them bring it in the house."

"That's a good idea." Emily went into the kitchen and put on a kettle of water for tea.

"Back in a jiff," Daniel called, his voice raised in excitement as the door banged shut again.

With each passing day, Daniel was growing stronger. His recurrence of leukemia had caused him to miss quite a bit of school last year, but Emily, Faith, and Josh had managed to help him stay on course with all of his classes so he didn't have to repeat sixth grade.

"Hey, Mom! This is Merry Hart and her mom."

"Reagan."

"I'm Emily. Y'all come on in." Meredith's eyes widened, and Emily realized she'd slipped back into her old way of speech. She'd just about broken herself of that habit, but every once in a while… "We're from Texas, and I haven't quite gotten it all out of my system yet."

Meredith spoke up. "Oh, no. You shouldn't do that. Get it out of your system, I mean. Daniel says it all the time, and I've heard people at school talking about how cool it is. I think it is too."

"Well, thank you, Meredith. You just earned yourself some oatmeal chocolate chip cookies. That is, if you like them."

"I love them!"

Daniel piped up. "Is it okay if we go upstairs and start working on the history thing? We have a lot to do before we can hand it over to Landon, and it's due next Tuesday."

"Of course. Just leave the door open."

"I know the rules, Mom," Daniel said, resisting the urge to roll his eyes and darting up the stairs. "Come on up, Merry! I have everything else we need for the project upstairs."

"I'm glad you have rules," Reagan said as she picked up the mug of chai that Emily set in front of her. She looked down at the hot liquid as the steam rose and warmed her face. "I'm new at this parenting thing since Meredith is an only child…and I'm doing it by myself. Her father and I are divorced." Reagan glanced over at Emily. How would a pastor's wife take the news that her son had made friends with a girl from a divorced family? But Emily's expression didn't change. It still held that welcoming smile that had greeted them at the door, and Reagan was relieved. She didn't want her daughter's family situation to stand in the way of anything good in her life. "Meredith's a good kid, always been easy, but I know things change as they get older. I was concerned when she came home from school the first day and told me she'd made guy friends but no girl friends. My first thought was, *I'm not ready for this.*"

Emily leaned over, placed her hand momentarily on Reagan's, and gave it a slight squeeze. "I think you can relax. Daniel and his friends Landon and Michael are really good kids, and we know Landon's and Michael's parents. They also have a couple of girls who hang out with them sometimes. As far as I know, they would be good friends for Meredith too. We know Molly's parents because they live in the Cove and attend WCCC."

"WCCC?"

"Oh, I'm sorry. So used to shortening it. That's Wentworth Cove Community Church. My husband's been pastor there for a year and a half. We moved here from Dallas."

"Ah. So you know what it's like to not know who to trust your kid with."

"I was so overly protective of Daniel when we first moved here that I made his older sister Faith go to every session with him and a guy who was giving him photography lessons. Of course, that turned out to be a good thing because Faith and Josh are married now, and we couldn't be happier to have him in the family."

"It sounds like the move to Maine was good for you and your family."

"It was. We've settled in here and are happy we came. Last winter took a little getting used to, but summers here more than make up for it. But you're already used to cold winters, so that won't be an adjustment you have to make. Did you say you've already found a job? That didn't take long."

"I have David Norsworthy to thank for that. He knew someone across the street from the art gallery who needed help in her bookstore."

"Maggie. She's a sweetheart. You'll enjoy working there. I hear the bookstore's been pretty busy lately."

"I started on Wednesday, and it's been a fairly slow week. I'm glad. I didn't want to be bombarded before I'd familiarized myself with the inventory, but on the other hand, I hope business picks up because I need the job. I'm a painter, but the paintings I sell won't be enough to live on. I had a part-time job at an art gallery in New York City."

"Daniel tells me you're living up at Lonewild."

"Yes, we really lucked into that at just the right time."

"Maybe it wasn't luck at all."

"What do you mean?"

"I think God might have had a hand in it. He takes care of us when we aren't always able to. I can think of so many times in my life when he scooped me up and set me down in just the right place at just the right time."

Reagan didn't respond immediately. She and Ryan hadn't grown up going to church, so the idea that someone would take care of you like your dad was supposed to seemed foreign. Her dad had not done that, so she hadn't grown up expecting it. Her friends' dads, on the other hand, were different. She'd seen them bail their daughters out of many sticky situations. She had always turned to Ryan, but since they'd gone to different colleges, she'd had to mostly fend for herself since high school graduation.

"I don't know. Maybe." It was all she could muster, and she felt guilty for not being able to converse on the subject.

"You're welcome to stay as long as the kids need to work, but if you have something else you need to do, I'll be happy to bring Meredith home in an hour or two. And if they need to finish the project tomorrow, she's more than welcome to come back. In fact, I could pick her up. I know where Lonewild is. Been there a few times to visit Miss Carter. Naming houses was something we had to get used to when we moved from Texas. Apparently it's quite a thing here."

"Well…"

"Would you like to go upstairs and check on the kids? See how the project is coming along? I'll take them some more cookies. That can be our excuse."

"Sure." Emily seemed to be able to read Reagan's thoughts—her hesitancies—and respond to them in a most reassuring way.

"That way you might feel more comfortable about leaving her here if they need more time. Come on in the kitchen and help me get some cookies and a couple of glasses of milk."

"Hey, Mom! Look at this cool poster Merry just finished," Daniel offered as Emily and Reagan entered his room. "She's a good artist, isn't she? I'm going to take a picture of it, and it will be one of our slides for the slide show Landon is making from our research."

"That's definitely a work of art, Meredith. It seems you've inherited your mother's talent."

"Thank you. I like history and art both, so this is a way to put my two favorite subjects together."

"Thanks for the cookies and milk, Mom. We need to work some more, though. You're not going to take Merry home now, are you, Mrs. Hart?"

"Mere, Mrs. Parker has offered to let you stay a little longer and bring you home later. Would you like that?" Reagan asked her daughter.

"Sure. If it's okay with you. We need to get all of this to Landon by Sunday so he'll have time to put it together because we have to present it to the class on Tuesday."

"I'll have her home by six, Reagan. And if they need to work tomorrow, I'll be happy to pick her up."

"I work tomorrow from twelve to five and I was going to take her with me. I'm sure she'd rather spend some time here. That is, if you really don't mind."

"What if I pick her up at one and bring her back to the bookstore by four?"

"Is that okay, Mom? Five hours at a bookstore sounds really boring. And I don't have that much homework, so what would I do?" Meredith responded, her eyes helping plead her case.

"I guess that'll be okay. I know you don't want to let down the group by not doing your part."

"Thanks, Mrs. Hart. We can get it all finished tomorrow," Daniel assured her.

Daniel couldn't be more polite, and Emily was so nice and welcoming, but Reagan hadn't been able to completely let her guard down. The thought of Jared somehow locating them was the stuff nightmares were made of, and she'd had her share of them lately.

Chapter Nine

Jared Loper had been staying with his old friend Al for a week but hadn't had any luck finding a way to support himself. And he didn't feel he could occupy Al's couch for long, so he was getting antsy. So far no one was even willing to interview him. He'd tried two medical equipment sales firms, a restaurant supply company, and a courier service. The possibility he had feared—that no one was willing to take a chance on an ex-con—was becoming a reality. A few more days of searching, and he would have to lower himself to what he'd done in college. Restaurants were always looking for experienced servers, and surely he could find one that wouldn't hold his prison record against him.

Jared looked down at Felix, asleep at his feet. The dog had taken a particular liking to him and had appointed himself Jared's protector by abandoning his dog bed in Al's room and taking up residence in the living room. Jared had never been what he'd refer to as a "dog person," but since he was somewhat bereft of friends, a loyal dog was better than nothing.

His mind took him back to a time when Meredith was about four years old and had begged him for a dog. "You don't need a dog. We don't have a yard, and if we had a dog he'd have to be walked. You're too young to walk a dog by yourself, I'm too busy, I don't think your mom would want to walk a dog three times a day, and dog walkers are expensive. So no. We're not getting a dog. One of these days when you're old enough to walk a dog by yourself, we'll talk about it again." But he knew that would be several years, and he was hoping she'd forget by then.

"Dog walkers are expensive," he'd told her. Dog walkers are expensive. *Dog walkers are expensive.*

"Hey, Al. Want me to walk Felix?"

"Sure. That would be great, buddy. I'm kind of tied up on the computer right now, and he hasn't been out this morning."

Jared had seen guys walking four and five dogs at a time. And he assumed they had their own business. No boss to report to. No embarrassing questions to have to answer on a job application. All he'd need would be a recommendation or two. Al would be one. He was sure he could get at least one or two more from friends or relatives who'd want to help him gain his independence back. If he had to stoop to calling his dad…well, so be it. He needed to find out what Reagan had done with his clothes anyway. He was getting tired of borrowing T-shirts and jackets from Al.

Not that he had a lot of clothes, since he'd mostly worn scrubs in his previous life, but he did have some nice evening wear, including a couple of expensive tuxes, and some golf outfits. He toyed with the idea of selling the tuxedoes on consignment and keeping the sportswear in case he did follow through with his idea of dog walking.

He'd need to have some business cards printed and put them in veterinarian offices and pet supply stores. But first…he needed a phone. It hadn't been easy to get by for even a week without one. He'd had to put Al's number on job applications…and that was humiliating.

If only his half of the divorce settlement hadn't gone to child support. But that was depleted now, so he'd have to do something soon if he was to have any self-respect at all.

"Felix and I are leaving for a few," he called to Al, who was busy doing who-knows-what in the other room.

Jared grabbed Felix's leash and attached it to his collar. How hard could it be to walk a dog? Even two or three or four?

Let's put this to the test. "How about a little research walk, Felix? You okay with that, boy?"

Jared and Felix hadn't been out ten minutes when Jared spotted a man who looked to be about his age walking four medium-sized dogs. The man was dressed in jeans and a sweatshirt, and Jared made a mental note that his new business wardrobe wouldn't have to break the bank. If he could sell both of his tuxes at a consignment shop, he could probably buy three or four pairs of jeans and a few shirts. Al had already given him one of his old jackets. He'd still need a phone, some business cards, boots for snow, and a heavier winter jacket.

Changing his brisk walk to almost a run, Jared caught up with the dog walker. "Hey, buddy. Mind if I ask you a quick question? I'm Jared, by the way."

"Sam. No. Go ahead."

"Are you a professional dog walker?"

"Sure am. Do you need help with your Rottweiler? I don't have any availability, but I might be able to find you someone."

"Oh, no. Temporarily out of work and just thinking about taking up dog walking myself. I was wondering how hard it is to get clients."

"Let's just say you jumped on board at the right time. I'm having to turn people away. I could send a couple your way to get you started if you're interested."

"Much appreciated, man. I'm new in town and getting a new phone and a new number tomorrow. How could I get in touch with you?"

"Here's my business card. Give me a holler when you're ready to start. Do you have any plastic bags in your pocket?"

"No. Why?"

"*Why?*" Sam looked at Jared incredulously.

"Oh." He grinned. "Felix and I left the apartment in sort of a hurry."

"Here's a couple. That's an essential in this business."

"Sure. I wasn't thinking. Thanks, man. Sam, right?"

"Sam White."

"Jared Loper. I'll be in touch," he said, stuffing Sam's business card and the plastic bags into his jacket pocket.

All five dogs were getting restless and one of Sam's dogs kept getting in Felix's personal space, so Jared decided to cross the street and head back to Al's. It would take a little bit of preparation, but Jared thought it was fortuitous that Sam would be able to send him some ready-made clients. Maybe, just maybe, his luck was beginning to take a turn for the better.

Back at the apartment, Jared punched in his dad's number on Al's phone. Letting go of one's pride was never easy, but it was hitting him particularly hard after the way he and his dad had ended things.

"Dad, it's Jared. I was wondering if you know what Reagan did with my clothes." Short and to the point. He didn't want to make small talk—afraid he might say something his dad would take offense to again—and he needed a favor, so he was taking great care to keep the conversation strictly business.

"They're here. Would you like me to bring them to you?"

Apparently his dad was not going to try to get him to move back home. Jared could feel the chill in his voice.

"That's fine, or I can come get them. Never mind. I wouldn't have a way to get them back here. I would appreciate it if you would bring them to Al's. I can give you his address."

"Third option. You could come to the house for a while, and then I could take you and the clothes back to Al's...if that's what you still want." A little less chilly, Jared thought. Maybe now would be a good time to bring up his plan to get a cell phone.

"Sure. That'll work. If you don't mind."

"Around three o'clock okay?"

"Yeah. I'll text you the address when we hang up. I'll meet you on the street so you won't have to park."

"Good idea. See you then, son."

Son. It was a good sign. Surely his dad would want to help him get a cell phone so he could start a dog-walking business.

As he stood on the sidewalk waiting for his father to arrive, Jared felt faintly like a schoolboy waiting for the bus to take him to kindergarten or first grade. Gone was his independence. Gone was his money. Gone was the bravado he'd had as a young, successful anesthesiologist. Gone were his wife and daughter.

He knew he could recoup the money, the independence, and maybe even the feeling of having the world by the tail. But would he ever be able to win his wife and daughter back? He simply had to and was willing to strive to that end...even if it meant working twelve-hour days to build up his new business. And he felt that if he played his cards right, he might be able to get his dad to help him with the startup.

Finding Reagan and Meredith was another hurdle, but he had an idea up his sleeve. It would, however, have to take a backseat to the dog-walking business because it would involve some outlay of money, and he knew without a doubt that his dad would not fund his search.

The twenty-minute ride to the house was uncomfortable for Jared since neither he nor his father was in a talkative mood—each afraid of saying something that would make the other angry or uncomfortable. A little small talk, but that was it. Jared took the opportunity to silently rehearse how he planned to approach the subject of his business idea and his need for a cell phone.

When they finally arrived at the house where Jared had spent most of his childhood and teen years, a wave of nostalgia swept over him. Something he wasn't expecting, and it almost caused him to choke up.

"House looks the same," he managed to get out.

"Yeah. I didn't want to change anything after your mom died. I'll leave it the way she liked it as long as I live here."

"What do you mean—as long as you live here? Are you planning on going somewhere?"

"Not particularly. Not any time soon anyway. But you never know what the future holds."

"There are a lot of good memories here. I'd hate to see you sell it."

"Let's don't worry about that now," Henry said, obviously eager to change the subject. "How've you been? How's Al? Want something to drink?"

"No thanks. Al's doing okay. He's a day trader. Seems to make pretty good money. I guess he's done his homework."

"And you? Any job prospects?"

Jared had played this scene in his mind many times in the past few hours.

Dad, I'm going into the dog walking business.

You're what?

I can't get an interview because of my prison record, so I'm going to start my own business.

Dog walking? Why that?

For several reasons. I'll be my own boss. I can make money and start getting my life back. I won't have to rely on Al much longer for a place to stay.

You don't have to rely on him now. Why don't you move back home?

I want to be independent. I need to be independent.

Okay, fine. But dog walking? Can't you do something with a little more, uh…prestige?

Not until I'm able to prove myself. Prove to people that I can overcome my past and make it on my own. I've done some soul searching since I've been at Al's. I messed up, but I don't have to give up. So I plan to fight my way back…whatever it takes.

Fine, son, but can't you come up with something besides dog walking?

That's the reaction he fully expected, but he decided he might as well jump right in as they entered the kitchen and sat down at the antique oak table. How many times had they, as a small family unit, sat around this same table and discussed the day's happenings? His day at school, his dad's lectures and book writing sessions, his mom's charity drives or garden club activities. He'd known for a while that those times were gone, but the thought had never hit home so hard as it did now. Gone also was the possibility of having that same type of life with Reagan and Meredith. Provided, of course, he could find them and persuade them to forgive him. To give him another chance. It was a long shot, but he hadn't completely given up.

He managed to bring his mind back to the business at hand. First things first. Lay his cards on the table and see how his dad responded.

"I'm going into the dog walking business."

"That's an interesting choice. How did you come up with that?" Henry asked.

Definitely *not* the response he'd expected. Where was the guilt trip?

"Well, Al has a dog, Felix. A Rottweiler. He sort of took to me, and I've been walking him occasionally. While we were out, I ran into a guy who was walking four dogs. We started talking, and I realized there was real money to be made. He even said he could send some clients my way and gave me his card." Jared nervously adjusted in his chair.

"That's great, son. When will you start? Do you need anything to help you get started?"

"You mean you think it's okay?" Jared asked, surprised at this positive response. His dad didn't seem to have any reservations at all.

"Of course. Why wouldn't I? It shows ingenuity and the willingness to take a chance with something new. I think it would be a good way to get back on your feet, and you never know what opportunities it might lead to. Did you use Al's phone to call me?"

"Yes."

"You'll need a phone for sure. I can help you with that. How about if I pay for six months, then you can take over the payments after that? Do you think that will give you enough time to build up the business?"

His father's offer took him off-guard. "That…yeah…" He faltered. "That would be great. I'm sure I can easily take over the payments in six months. That's a…a very generous offer."

"Of course. How about some business cards? You'll need to get some printed, but they're not expensive. You can order them online."

"That would be very helpful. Thanks. I'll pay you back. I'm going to sell some clothes on consignment. I probably won't be needing tuxes any time soon."

"I'm not worried about that, but if it'll make you feel better—"

"I want to."

"Fine. I believe in you and I'm proud of you for thinking of this, but you never really seemed interested in dogs."

"I guess Felix won me over. He doesn't care about anything but walks, food, and scratches behind the ears. Never asks me where I've been or what I've been doing for seven years."

"I know you want to get started as soon as possible, so let's load the clothes in the car and get you a phone. Here's money for some business cards," Henry said, handing Jared a couple of fifties.

"I'll pay—"

"That's fine. We can discuss that later. I just want you to get on your feet and settle in as soon as possible. New York City isn't the most inexpensive place one can live. Have you thought about relocating?"

"Relocating? I've been here my whole life. I wouldn't know how to live anywhere else. Why are you bringing it up?"

"I just thought you might be able to become independent sooner if your living expenses weren't so high."

"You said you weren't planning on selling the house any time soon, but it sounds like you've toyed with the idea of leaving. Are you planning to retire soon and move out of the city?"

"There's plenty of time to talk about that later, but right now let's go get you a phone."

Something about the way Henry kept changing the subject concerned Jared. Something was going on with his dad, but he couldn't put his finger on it.

"How'd your afternoon go with your dad?" Al asked when Jared returned to the apartment.

"Better than I expected. He offered to pay my phone bill for six months. I know you'll be happy I don't have to keep using yours. Having one almost makes me feel normal again. Isn't it crazy how dependent we get on those things? It's like having the whole world in your pocket. The whole world except my family, that is."

"About that…"

"About what?"

"I've been doing a little detective work."

"And? Spill it, man. Do you know where they are?"

"Hold on. I didn't say that."

"But you know something. What is it?"

"I might be close to finding her. Maybe not. Time will tell."

"What do you know? Don't keep me in suspense."

"Was she a painter?"

"Reagan? No. All she did was grow herbs and vegetables and cook and go out to lunch with her friends. Well…and take care of Meredith." After a short pause he continued. "I'll have to admit she was a really great mother. I'm sure she still is. Why do you ask?"

"I found a Reagan Loper on the internet. She's a painter and she has a website. Her picture's not on it though. And no bio. Just photos of her paintings and info on how to buy them. She's really good."

"That can't be Reagan. I would have known if she was into art. Wouldn't I? I mean, I guess she could have picked it up as a hobby after she divorced me. Are they any good?"

Al shrugged and walked toward the bedroom. "I'm not an art critic, but I imagine she sells a few here and there. Want to see?"

"Sure," Jared said, following him to the desk that housed his computer.

"Plus—"

"Yeah?"

"I have an idea," Al said, his fingers clicking on the keyboard. "Here it is. What do you think?" He turned the computer around so Jared could have a full view.

"I guess those are good. Not my taste, but I'm sure some people would find them interesting enough to buy. I'll admit it's not a common name, but I have a hard time believing Reagan went in that direction. I thought if she had to get a job it would be at a bakery or something like that. Something to do with food. Not painting. She never mentioned anything about wanting to paint when we were married."

"People change."

"I guess I couldn't blame her," Jared admitted. "She was embarrassed. She made that pretty obvious during the trial. But you said you had an idea. Spit it out."

"Do you remember my sister in Pennsylvania? Charlotte?"

"The one with seven kids?"

"Can you believe it? How opposite can siblings be, eh?"

"What about her?"

"I was thinking she could order a painting—the cheapest one—and then see where it shipped from. Reagan doesn't know her and wouldn't suspect someone from a different state."

"Al, my man, you're a genius. But I thought you didn't think I should look for her."

"What can I say? I got bored."

Chapter Ten

On Sunday afternoon Brett pulled his car up in the driveway at Lonewild, rolled down the window, killed the engine, and looked at his watch. Fifteen minutes early again. He was going to have to stop these early arrivals, or Reagan might get the idea he was interested in her as more than a renter of his aunt's house. He'd tried to convince himself he wasn't—that this was only a mild curiosity about a mysterious lady who, by the way, was single…and more than slightly attractive.

He'd talked David into helping him move Meredith's bedroom furniture upstairs and mulled going inside before David got there but thought better of it. If he stayed in his car, maybe David would think he'd just arrived. He hoped that anyway, or he'd never hear the end of it.

"Brett?" a voice, familiar now, called from the kitchen window. "Meredith said she heard someone in the driveway. Come on in."

"I'm a little early and didn't want to disturb you in case you weren't ready for us."

"That's okay. I made blueberry muffins, and you can get a jump on David because I know he likes them."

"Well, in that case…" Brett said as he made his way to the side door, a door he had entered so many times after he'd moved in with his grandparents. He'd spent almost as much time with his Aunt Ida at Lonewild as he had with them.

On that stormy spring night twenty-three years ago, his parents were traveling home to Augusta from a company party in Portland when his dad—who was driving too fast and who Brett now suspected had had too much to drink—lost control of the car, veered into oncoming traffic, and hit another car head on. Both of his parents were killed on impact. The only person in the other car, a teenage boy on his way home from a date, was left a paraplegic. His grandparents hadn't told him, but he'd overheard them talking and was old enough to understand what had happened.

He'd often wondered what happened to that boy, who would be only five years older than Brett. Was he able to finish high school, go to college, get a job, marry, have children? He knew he shouldn't, but for some insane reason, he felt guilty every time his mind went there. It was illogical. He had nothing to do with his dad's excessive drinking, but there it was. And he hadn't been able to shake it all these years.

"Brett?" Reagan's voice jarred him out of his trance as he stood on the steps at the side door. "Are you coming in? The muffins are still hot…fresh out of the oven." Just then David and Elizabeth pulled up behind Brett's car. "Oops. Too late to get a jump on David. He who hesitates is not only lost but doesn't get to eat as many blueberry muffins."

But also doesn't get teased by David for arriving at the house fifteen minutes early, thought Brett, as he pried his hand off the door knob and entered the kitchen. It hadn't smelled this good in ages. In her younger years, Ida had been quite a cook. Lately, though, as her eyesight faded, she'd cooked less and less. It was nice to smell Lonewild again as he remembered it from his youth. Reagan had breathed new life into it.

"Brett, you haven't met my daughter. This is Meredith."

Brett gave an imaginary hat tip. "Nice to meet you, Meredith."

"Thank you for moving my bedroom furniture upstairs. I love your house."

"It's actually my aunt's house. I just help her take care of it. But I'm glad you like it."

"Hey, everybody," David said as he and Elizabeth entered the kitchen. "Do I smell muffins?"

"You do indeed. Grab one and put some butter on it while it's still warm. Hi, Elizabeth. I didn't know you were coming too. You'd better get in on this before the guys finish them off."

"Sure. Figured there would be something I could do. Maybe while David and Brett are moving furniture out, we can move your art things into your new studio."

"That's a great idea. That way I can start painting tomorrow. Brett, I want to ask you something while I'm thinking about it. I wondered if you and Miss Carter would mind if I plant some herbs in the backyard this spring. Maybe even a very small vegetable garden. I love to cook, and it's hard to find organic and locally sourced vegetables here. Not that it was easy in the city, but I had a sizable patio garden. I'm going to put a few pots of herbs in the kitchen window and the solarium during the winter. It's so exciting to have all this lovely space now, and I would love to take advantage of it."

"She paints. She cooks. She sells books. She grows her own food. Is there anything you can't do?" Brett said, hoping he didn't sound too impressed. David would never let him live it down.

"She can't drive very well on snow," Meredith chipped in.

Meredith's remark elicited laughter from everyone, and Reagan said, "She's right. I can't, but I'm sure I'll get a lot of practice this winter. I can't seem to open this window either. It's not locked. Is there a trick?"

"I think the trick might be that you're not pulling up on it hard enough," Brett said as he pried the window open, letting in the cool ocean breeze. "And in answer to your question about a garden in the spring, I'm sure Aunt Ida would love it if you did that. She was quite a cook herself in her heyday. Between her and my grandmother, I ate very well growing up. I miss that."

"Brett, did you just try to wangle a home cooked meal from Reagan?" David asked, cocking one eyebrow.

"Well, it's either that or she's going to have to buy me surf and turf for moving this furniture," he quipped as he gave Reagan a sideways glance and a grin. "Just kidding. Inside joke, David."

After forty-five minutes of moving and arranging furniture, Reagan said, "That's great, guys. Meredith and I appreciate it so much, don't we, Mere?"

"Yes. Thank you. I'm gonna love it upstairs. We've never lived in a two-story house before."

"Actually, we've never lived in a house before," Reagan added. "Always apartments. So this is a real change for us."

"I was looking at the paint job on the house when I drove up," Brett said, "and the paint's chipped and worn off in a lot of places. I think it's time for a fresh coat. I'll call around and arrange to get someone out here before the weather gets bad. I'll give him your number so he can co-ordinate with you…that is, if you don't mind."

"What color?" Reagan asked.

"Well, it's been white as long as I've known it. So I guess white again."

"Um…" Reagan hesitated.

"What?"

"Since you're going to have it repainted anyway…"

"Yeah? What's on your mind?"

"Would you consider a different color? Do you think your aunt would mind? White's kind of like vanilla ice cream. Why would you order that when you could have Rocky Road or Mocha Almond Fudge? When it snows, you've got a white house and white everything else. No contrast."

"Spoken like a true artist. What do you suggest?"

"What about either Wedgewood blue or dark red? Green would blend in too much with the trees. Or yellow. Pale yellow would be nice."

"I could go with the blue if it's not too dark or bright, but let me run it by Aunt Ida. If she okays it, I'll bring you some paint samples."

"Wedgewood blue," Reagan explained.

"I'm supposed to know what that is?" Brett asked, laughing.

"Don't worry, Brett," Elizabeth said. "It's a very pretty color. Light and subdued. Not bright at all. I think it would look good."

"I'm not an expert on color nuances, so I'll take the advice of the ladies on this one."

"Thanks for being open about it," Reagan said.

"I know Aunt Ida wanted someone who really cared about Lonewild to live here, and obviously you do, so…Wedgewood blue it is."

Reagan loved Lonewild. Everything about it, from the spacious solarium where she could grow herbs and vegetables in the winter to her new downstairs studio made possible by Miss Carter's generous offer to let them use the two upstairs bedrooms. In the past when Ryan would come to the city for more than a day, Meredith would bunk with her mom and Ryan would occupy Meredith's room. Now, Reagan had plans to make a guest room out of the fourth bedroom. Another bonus gained by being able to expand to the upstairs.

"What just happened?" Elizabeth asked her husband when they were in the car.

"Your guess is as good as mine. Probably better."

"He's obviously interested. You know him better than I do. Is this normal behavior for him?"

"No. He's smitten," David said as he turned onto Shore Road. "I just hope he doesn't go too fast and get his heart broken again. Reagan's nothing like Erica, but still…I don't know if she's ready."

"I think they both might have trust issues. Understandably so. Maybe they've worked through them, but what if they haven't?"

"They're adults and we'll have to leave it up to them. Promise me you won't say anything to Reagan. We need to keep our noses out of it, even if we're tempted."

"Of course I won't, but I don't want this to turn into an awkward situation. Lonewild is so perfect for her and Meredith, and I wouldn't want anything between Brett and Reagan to change that. Maybe we're jumping to conclusions here, though."

"I don't think so, Elizabeth. I've known Brett since junior high, and I'd be willing to bet he has a crush. Inside jokes and painting the house blue, for goodness' sake," he said, shaking his head.

Monday morning after Reagan had dropped Meredith off at school, she dialed Brett's number. "Are you busy? I'm sorry to bother you at work, but I didn't know when was a good time to call."

"No. This is fine. Everything okay?"

"I didn't want to mention it while David was here yesterday, but I sold one of Miss Carter's paintings on my website for seventy-five dollars. I think we should have prints made before I ship it. What do you think? They would probably sell for somewhere between twenty-five and forty-five. Maybe only ten or fifteen prints for each original?"

"Really? That was super fast."

"Right? It was up only a couple of days."

"Yeah. If you think you can sell that many, go for it. Do you know of a place that makes prints?"

"David will know. He'll think it's for me," Reagan assured him. "I'll ask him today. Do you want me to send you the seventy-five dollars?"

"Do you think you'd have time to run it by to Aunt Ida? I think it would make a bigger impact coming from you. She'll probably be surprised. Also, the last time I talked to her, she mentioned wanting to meet your daughter. She's always had a fondness for kids. Pity she never married and had her own…but she doted on me, so I guess I'm glad I could help fill that void in her life."

"Sure. Mere has a big group presentation in history class tomorrow, so she should be freed up a bit after that. We'll go by in the next few days."

"Great. And let me know how much the prints will be when you find a place to do them. There should be one in Kennebunk or Kennebunkport. If not, try Portland and Augusta. I'll foot the bill for that, and you can pay me back when they sell."

"I don't suppose you've had a chance to ask your aunt about painting the house blue since we just talked about it yesterday?" Since Brett had mentioned it, Reagan couldn't keep from thinking about how good the house would look with a fresh coat of blue paint.

"No, but if you want, you can do that when you take her the money this week. Artist to artist. She'll probably understand Wedgewood blue better than I do. But who wouldn't, huh?"

Reagan stared out the car window at the colors of late fall, still sometimes unable to believe the beauty of this quaint village. "I'm not going to touch that one since I'm at your mercy while living in your aunt's house. I'll let you know what she says about the blue, though."

"Oh, while I'm thinking about it, you won't believe what she's done now."

"What?"

"Well, she didn't like the fact that a retirement home was named Sundown—I can see her point—so...she talked management into changing it. Can you believe that? They're actually going to change the name of the facility."

"Are you serious? I did get the feeling she could be pretty persuasive. What are they changing it to?"

"It's still in the talking stages with the board of directors, but probably either Sunrise or Sunshine Assisted Living Center."

Reagan was growing rather fond of her landlady. A woman who was inspired to take up painting at an advanced age. Who apparently served as the counselor and therapist for all of Wentworth Cove. And who didn't mind taking on an entire board of directors to effect change she believed in. Reagan had apparently been an inspiration for Ida Carter, but in Reagan's mind, Ida was the inspiration.

Chapter Eleven

Halloween had come and gone with nothing to remember it for except a Fall Festival at the church where Daniel's dad was minister. The Parkers had offered to pick up Meredith, and she was excited to have something social that wasn't school related. Reagan stayed home in case any trick-or-treaters made a visit to Lonewild. According to Brett, when his Aunt Ida lived there, children came in droves because she always put on some sort of costume and sat outside with huge buckets of candy. She loved the happy shrieks of the children whose parents would bring them by the carloads.

Reagan had no Halloween visitors, however. Word apparently had gotten out that Miss Carter was no longer living there, so they felt no reason to go to Lonewild this year. Reagan wasn't disappointed. She was in no hurry to start attracting people to her temporary abode. If people didn't ask questions, she didn't have to provide answers. And that was fine with her. Would there ever be a time again when she wasn't afraid to be transparent? To open up to the curiosity of people who wondered what had brought someone who'd lived in New York City all her life to Wentworth Cove, Maine?

Ryan was supposed to drive up from Boston for the weekend, and both she and Meredith were so excited about his visit. It had been much too long since she'd seen her brother, and she had so much to tell him, to show him. He'd never been to Wentworth Cove, and Reagan wondered if he would like it. If he'd think she had made a good decision. She hoped he would because she usually ran things by him first, but she'd done this on her own without asking his advice.

Still deep in thought about Ryan's visit, Reagan pulled her car into the parking spot behind Bernard's Books and Collectibles and went in for her four-hour shift. She'd become comfortable in her new part-time job and didn't mind when Maggie took a long lunch break and left her in charge of the shop.

"Good morning," Maggie said. "Ready for a new week? It's supposed to be really cold this week, and we might have some snow. I don't know about you, but I'm ready for it. There's always something really special about the first big snow that covers everything and lasts for a while. It's just so beautiful."

"I'm ready for everything except snow-covered roads. I'm a novice when it comes to driving on snow. Did I say *novice*? I meant *coward*."

"The snowplows come around often. Usually the main roads and streets are clean."

"Then it's just my driveway I have to worry about. And that's kind of long."

"Maybe you should invest in a snow blower."

"That's probably a good idea. And Maggie?"

"Yes?"

"I was wondering if I could have Saturday off. My brother's coming for a visit, and I haven't seen him in ages. I'd like to show him around the area."

"Your twin, right? Of course. Take the day off and enjoy the visit."

"Thanks. I'd like you to meet him too. Do you mind if I bring him by the shop?"

"Sure. Any brother of yours is a brother of mine."

That's not exactly what I had in mind, but it's a start, Reagan thought.

Just then Reagan's phone rang. Who would be calling her at work, she wondered. She took it out of her jacket pocket and saw Brett's name pop up. No customers were in the shop, so she answered it before it could roll over to voice mail.

"This is Reagan."

"Sorry to call you at work, but I had dialed your number before I realized how late it was. If it's a problem, you can call me back."

"We don't have any customers yet, so no problem. You're not calling to kick us out of Lonewild, are you? I really hope not because I'm looking forward to living in a pretty blue house."

"Yeah, Aunt Ida told me she'd talked to you and to go ahead with it. I think she was pleased about the new color. She wants to see it when we get it done. She was also pleased, and surprised, that you'd sold one of her watercolors. She didn't expect it...and so soon. But that's not why I called. I heard the coast is supposed to get some frigid weather and a big snow this week, so I'm going to bring you a snow blower for the driveway. I'll get one that's lightweight. It'll be easy to handle. I remember Meredith said driving in the snow isn't one of your many talents."

"You don't have to do that, Brett. I was planning to buy one as soon as I could figure out where to get it."

"Easier for me to find a good one in Augusta, and this way you won't have to go into Kennebunk or Portland."

"That's very thoughtful. I'll pay you for it."

"Not necessary. We'll just say it's part of the house and you're leasing it."

"Fair enough. I appreciate it."

"Done and done. I'll pick one up this afternoon. I'm planning to drive in to see Aunt Ida tomorrow anyway. Want me to bring it to you at work or at the house? If I come to the house after you get off, I can show you how to use it. Not that you couldn't figure it out by yourself."

"I pick up Mere from school at three-thirty, so I'll be home by four. But if you're feeling daring, why don't you come by around five or five-thirty. I was planning to try my hand at clam chowder. I've never made it before, but if you're not afraid—"

"Are you kidding? Brett Mason hasn't been known to turn down a home-cooked meal in…well…ever. Deal. Five would be great if that's not too early. I don't want to be late getting back to Augusta, and it's an hour and a half drive."

"No. Five's fine. See you then." Reagan put her phone back in her pocket and tried to act nonchalant so that Maggie wouldn't start asking questions.

"Hmm. I heard only a couple of minutes of your end of that conversation," Maggie said, "but if I'm not mistaken, Mr. Brett Mason is taking care of his renter rather well. Bringing you a snow blower all the way from Augusta, I take it."

"He was coming to visit his aunt anyway tomorrow."

"Um hmm."

"Okay, I'm going to check inventory," Reagan said, shrugging her shoulders and smiling.

Reagan couldn't remember a time when blue wasn't her favorite color. There were always copious amounts of blue in her watercolors—blue skies, Eastern bluebirds, blue hydrangeas, blue and white china, the sea. The sea.

Another perk to living in Lonewild. Views of the Atlantic Ocean from one entire side of the house. And now she was living in a blue house. She and Ida had agreed on a muted shade of light Wedgewood blue, and the painters Brett had contracted to do the job were able to finish in three days...well before the winter storm was scheduled to hit.

She made a mental note to arrange a time that Ida could see it. Reagan was looking forward to having her out and hoped she would approve of the way she and Meredith were taking care of the house and property. Not much to do in the yard this time of year, but she had big plans for the spring. Already she found herself hoping to be able to stay at Lonewild longer than the twelve months her contract stated. As far as she was concerned, they had no reason to leave.

And, of course, Meredith felt the same way her mother did. She'd taken to the upstairs like a duck to water, decorating not only her new room, but also helping her mother turn the extra bedroom into a guest room for her uncle. And he was coming to occupy that room in a few days.

Both Reagan and Meredith couldn't wait to see him. It had been too long—much longer than their usual month apart. He'd been busier than usual with his architectural firm and hadn't been able to get away. But he was coming this weekend, and Reagan hoped he would be as positive about the move as she and Meredith were.

Chapter Twelve

On Thursday the snow came down softly and silently at first, and Reagan was able to drive Meredith to school with no problems. But by afternoon the wind was whistling through bare tree limbs, and snowflakes no longer floated lazily down but were propelled by the first bitter winds of approaching winter and beat against the windows of Lonewild.

On one hand, Reagan was glad she'd been able to quickly learn the ins and outs of her new snow blower for her long driveway, but on the other hand she wasn't so sure about the roads leading to Meredith's school. Her ringing phone interrupted her thoughts.

"Reagan, it's Elizabeth. I was wondering if you'd like me to bring Meredith home. The roads here in Kennebunk seem to be okay, but I'm not sure if the snowplows have made it to Wentworth Cove yet. My SUV is four-wheel drive and will go anywhere, so I'll be happy to bring her home."

"To be completely honest, I was beginning to feel a little apprehensive. I have that new snow blower, but I can't snow blow my way through all the streets between here and the school. I know I have to tackle this fear sometime, though."

"You don't have to tackle it today, so let me bring her. I don't mind at all."

"Okay. I appreciate it. I made a huge batch of clam chowder the other night. I'll send some home with you if you want it."

"You don't have to twist my arm. See you soon. It might be a good idea for you to call the school and tell them I'm picking her up."

"I'll do that as soon as we hang up."

After she spoke to the school secretary, Reagan looked out the window of her studio at the thickening, swirling flurry of snow and wondered if Ryan would be able to get from Boston to Lonewild the next day. He was supposed to arrive around four o'clock on Friday. Putting a photo of a winter scene she'd taken a couple of years ago on the edge of her easel, Reagan started to paint. The photo of a snow-covered Central Park made her a little nostalgic. All of her life had been spent in New York City, and the park had played a large part in both her childhood and adulthood.

Painting had always been therapeutic for Reagan, and she could use some therapy as she thought about the possibility that Ryan might not get to come after all. A lot was riding on this trip. She wanted to show him her new safe haven, introduce him to David, Elizabeth, and Maggie, and most of all just be in his presence.

Ryan Ellis pulled into the driveway at Lonewild at exactly four-thirty on Friday afternoon. Reagan and Meredith, both adorned in their warmest coats and snow boots, saw him from the kitchen window and raced outside to see who could get the first hug. He enveloped them both in his strong arms and walked them into the house without bringing in his bags. First things first.

"Uncle Ryan, it's been so long since we've seen you. You should have come sooner. We have so much to show you and so much to tell you."

"For goodness' sake, Mere, let him sit down. Or do you want to get the stuff out of your car first?" Reagan asked, setting a cup of coffee in front of him.

"That can wait. I just brought one bag and a couple of hang-ups. I'm not eager to go out into that bitter wind again quite yet. " Ryan sipped his hot drink and warmed his hands on the mug.

"We made a guest room for you upstairs. My bedroom's up there too. Miss Carter said at first we couldn't use the upstairs, but then she changed her mind. She's really nice. You'll like her. You want to meet her, right? And her nephew's nice too. His name's Brett. He helped us move my furniture upstairs. Do you like the house? We just had it repainted. Mom and Miss Carter decided on the color. She's a watercolor artist too. And, Uncle Ryan, you won't believe this."

"I won't believe what?" Ryan asked, laughing at his exuberant niece.

"Mom was the one who inspired her to start painting! I found her watercolors upstairs when we moved in. What a coincidence, huh? I'm sorry, Mom. Did you want to tell him that?"

Reagan refrained from telling Meredith that Ryan already knew everything she had been revealing. The siblings talked on the phone at least every other day, so there was very little that was actually news to him.

The one thing Reagan hadn't told him about was her landlady's nephew. He made a mental note to find out more about this Brett guy and wondered why his sister hadn't mentioned him.

"That's okay, Mere. I'll have plenty to tell him about my job at the bookstore and other things. Why don't you tell him about school and your new friends? Or would you like to give him a tour of the house first?"

"Do you want to see the rest of the house now, Uncle Ryan? It's so cool. You'll love it so much you might want to design one like it."

"I do want to see it. Let me grab my clothes out of the car, though. I think the wind has settled down a bit. I also want to hear about school and your friends, but we have all weekend. Maybe longer if this snow doesn't stop soon. I was lucky to be able to come at all. Fortunately, the major highways were clear. The only trouble I had was getting from the main road to your house."

"We have a snow blower. Brett bought it for us, but Mom has to use it often when it's coming down this fast, and we didn't know exactly when you were going to get here."

There was that name again. Brett. The more Meredith talked about him, the more Ryan wondered why Reagan hadn't mentioned him. It wasn't like her to keep anything from him. Especially someone who obviously was playing a major role in their lives here in Wentworth Cove. Moving furniture for them. Buying them a snow blower. He decided to shelve it for now, though, and talk to his sister about it when Meredith wasn't around. She might open up more.

Ryan grabbed his coat and gloves. "I'll be back in a minute. Then let's have that house tour."

By the time Ryan had had a thorough walk-through of Lonewild by his niece, he was convinced his sister had made the right decision. It seemed to be the perfect hideaway for Reagan and Meredith, and he was relieved they were both settling into the community. A part time job for Reagan and a new school with new friends for Meredith were icing on the cake.

Later that evening he had a chance to talk to his sister alone. "Rea, I'm really glad you made this decision. It feels right."

"We had to get away. You know that. Besides…I'm glad it put us closer to Boston. I know you don't have any clients up here, but you can easily run up for weekends pretty often, right?"

"Sure. I'd rather drive than navigate Logan and JFK any day. It wasn't that bad until I got to your road. And the fact that you'd blown most of the snow off the driveway helped." Ryan paused for a moment. "By the way, what's this I hear about the nephew of the landlady buying you a snow blower?"

Reagan hoped she wasn't blushing and that Ryan couldn't read her they way he usually could. "I offered to pay for it, but he said just consider it part of the house. I'll leave it with the house when I move. *If* I move, that is. We're pretty happy here. I know you can tell what Mere thinks of it."

"Right down her alley, isn't it? I'm convinced she's going to be a docent at a museum one of these days."

Reagan laughed. "Maybe. She and a couple of her new friends—guys, if you can believe that—earned an A plus on their history project. Only A plus in the class, and her friend Daniel said it was mostly because of her contributions to the project."

"That's great. I'm really proud of her for the way she's adjusted to this move. It could have been so different. I know she left some good friends back in the city. Any girls in the picture?"

"She's mentioned a couple, but so far her favorite seems to be a guy named Daniel. He was new here last year. I've met his mom, and his dad is the minister of the local community church."

"Have you gone?" Ryan asked.

"To the church? No, but they picked up Mere and took her to the Fall Festival social on Halloween."

"That's nice. How do you like your job?"

"I'm glad you asked. I want to take you there tomorrow and introduce you to my boss. I usually work on Saturdays, but she let me have the day off because you were coming."

"Sounds nice."

"She is. I think you'll like her." *I hope you like her because...well, I have a plan.*

"The main thing is that you like her...and that you don't mind not working in an art gallery. I know that's what you wanted when you moved here."

"Hey. Remember I told you about our landlady's watercolors? Well, I've sold a couple on my website."

"And the fact that your paintings inspired her to start painting. That's a pretty amazing coincidence."

"I'm beginning to believe there's no such thing as coincidence, but that's a conversation for another day. I'm just so glad you're here. It kind of seals this whole move—makes it seem real."

"Oh, it's real all right. Have you talked to Henry?" Ryan, as well as Reagan, had grown fond of Henry and Donna in the absence of their own parents. Now Donna was gone, and Henry was out of the picture too. Ryan understood it was risky. The more people who knew, the higher the chance Jared would be able to find them.

"No, and I feel bad about it. But what can I do? I trust him, but I can't afford to take any chances. Mere misses him, and I know he misses her."

"Maybe you could meet him somewhere in between. You know Jared can't leave New York, don't you? I imagine his parole officer is keeping a pretty close check on him."

"I know he's not *supposed* to, but you know as well as I that he can be pretty headstrong when he sets his mind to something."

"I guess you're right," Ryan conceded. "Maybe you shouldn't take any chances."

"Have you heard from Mom and Dad?" Reagan asked.

"No. You?"

"No. I guess they're not planning to come home for Christmas…again."

"We might as well quit wishing that, Rea. Not gonna happen. I'm sure they'll send the obligatory gifts, though."

"That reminds me. I have a few prints and originals that need to be mailed, and I don't really want to mail them from here. Would you mind taking them back and mailing them from Boston?"

"Sure. No problem. You're thinking of everything, aren't you?"

"I hope so."

Ryan stood. "I guess I'd better head upstairs to bed. What time do you want to get started in the morning?"

"No reason to leave early. Let's drop by the bookstore first. I want you to meet Maggie." Reagan caught herself smiling at the thought of her brother's reaction to her boss. "Then we can go across the street to see David and Elizabeth. Then I guess we'll just ride around the area. What do you think? Anything special you want to see?"

"Mere's school maybe."

"Yeah, I'm sure she'll want to show you that."

As Reagan was clearing the table, a ding from her phone caught her attention. Brett.

I was just wondering if the snow blower worked okay and your brother was able to navigate the road and driveway.

Ryan heard it too. "Everything okay?"

"Everything's fine. Just a friend checking on us."

"Maggie, this is my brother Ryan," Reagan announced as they entered Bernard's Books and Collectibles the next morning.

"Maggie Culwell. So nice to finally meet you, Ryan." She extended her hand.

Ryan's eyes were glued to the woman in front of him. His sister hadn't prepared him for this. When she talked about her boss who managed a used bookstore, he pictured a frumpy older woman with her hair pulled back in a bun and a pencil sticking through it—and wearing a black dress that came a couple of inches past her knees. But not this. Not a woman—about his age?—who could have, he thought, adorned the cover of any issue of *Vogue* magazine. A natural beauty, but a beauty nonetheless. Some women just didn't need makeup.

"Ryan?" Reagan brought him back to reality and he took Maggie's hand.

"I'm happy to meet you too," Ryan said. "Thank you for taking such good care of my little sister."

"I thought you and Reagan were twins."

"We are, but I'm five minutes older." It had always been a matter of some pride for Ryan for a reason his sister couldn't comprehend. But she was happy to let him crow about it whenever he wanted to.

"How long will you be here?" Maggie asked.

"Unfortunately, I have to leave tomorrow afternoon." *Unfortunate indeed*, he thought. "But I'll be back soon to stay longer. I had to come check out this Lonewild I'd been hearing so much about."

"I just wanted Ryan to meet you and see where I work, but we have a full day ahead of us, so we won't stay…since you have customers," Reagan said.

"So nice to meet you, Maggie. Maybe we'll have more time to visit the next time I'm in town." *Which might be even sooner than I'd planned,* Ryan thought.

"I'd really like that," Maggie said.

Chapter Thirteen

The more Jared thought about Al's plan to have his sister order a watercolor from Reagan's website, the more he liked the idea. Surely the package would be postmarked with the place of origination. That would be a start. He just hoped it wasn't all the way across the country in some place like California or Texas. It would be just like her to get as far away as possible, though, so he couldn't see his daughter easily even if he located them.

He'd found himself many times wondering what she looked like at twelve years of age. He tried to imagine her face like one of those age progression drawings of missing children. When she was five, she looked a lot like her mother. Did she still, he wondered.

Walking dogs had proved to be a good choice for Jared. Sam had sent four clients his way, and his business cards placed in veterinarian offices had netted him another four. Apparently there was quite a demand for dog walkers, especially as the weather was getting colder. While people in the city were used to walking, many of them worked and had to leave their dogs in an apartment all day. Most people wanted two thirty-minute walks a day, so Jared was beginning to get back on his feet and pay Al for continuing to live with him. He hoped to grow the business enough to be able to afford a place of his own soon. Maybe a small studio apartment. Something affordable. But as Henry had reminded Jared, "affordable" places were few and far between in New York City.

With Felix curled up at his feet, he called to Al who, as usual, was holed up in his bedroom. "I'm going to walk Felix, and when I get back, would you like me to order pizza before I do my afternoon walks?"

"Sure. That'd be great."

"And could we talk more about your sister ordering a painting from Reagan?"

"Yeah."

Jared and Felix had settled into a mutually satisfying routine of walking a couple of times a day before and after his rounds with the other dogs, and Al was spending more and more time in his bedroom—doing his trading, Jared assumed. Whatever it was, he was being secretive about it, but Jared didn't pry and Al didn't offer any explanations.

"Here's the money to send your sister for the cheapest print on Reagan's website," Jared said, handing Al a fifty and a twenty as they were scarfing down a large mushroom and pepperoni. "This should cover the painting and the shipping. I sure hope we're not spitting in the wind here, but I can't imagine two Reagan Lopers and I can't find another one on the internet."

"It has to be her. We'll track her down. Don't worry. The more I think about it, the more I realize you have every right to see your daughter."

"I appreciate it, man. Appreciate you letting me stay here too. I'll be out soon."

"No rush. You're not in my way, and Felix is getting special treatment from a professional dog walker."

"I was wondering… who's that other person who has paintings on Reagan's website? Can't remember her name now. Any ideas?"

"Yeah, I'm on it, man. I'll find out. And I'll text Charlotte to order that print tonight. Should know something soon."

"Thanks. I'm off to do my afternoon rounds and then distribute some more business cards to a few other places. Apartment buildings this time, I think."

"Sounds like a plan."

Now that Jared was getting back on his feet financially, he was ready to get on with reconnecting with his daughter. He felt as though his ex-wife had robbed him of seven years of her life. Reagan could have at least brought her to see him once in a while. Could have kept the lines of communication open even though he had no custodial rights. It wasn't fair, and he wasn't about to sweep it under the rug. He would right that wrong if it took him the rest of his life.

Chapter Fourteen

"Way to bury the lede, Brett." David wouldn't normally call Brett at work, but he'd discovered something and couldn't wait until he saw him again to get to the bottom of it.

"Bury the lede? What are you talking about?"

"You're a journalist. You know what 'bury the lede' means."

"Of course I do, but I have no idea what you're talking about."

"For all your talk about your aunt, you've never once mentioned that she was a watercolorist. You do realize I own an art gallery, don't you? We've known each other for what…twenty years? Why didn't you tell me?"

"It was her choice, not mine. She never thought she was good enough to sell any of her paintings. For her, it was just a way to fill her life with beauty and pleasure for the last few years. She never wanted or expected anyone else to see them. Had them stashed away upstairs at Lonewild. Of course, I knew. And when Reagan moved in, she saw them. I think Meredith spotted them first actually. Aunt Ida asked Reagan and me not to say anything. How did you find out? Did Reagan—" Brett didn't expect that Reagan had told David about the paintings, but then again, he didn't really know her that well either.

"No. Reagan never mentioned them, but I went to her website to look for a certain print we'd had at one time, and well...you can imagine my surprise when some paintings popped up that I didn't recognize. Looked more closely at the artist and couldn't believe my eyes. Have any sold?"

"Before I answer," Brett said, "you tell me something. What do you think of them? Are they any good?"

"Any good? I'd showcase them here without hesitation. Be honored to. Can you imagine the reception she'd get? Not only because they're good, but also because she's in many ways the matriarch of Wentworth Cove."

"Well..."

"Well what?"

"I'm not sure how to handle this since she made both of us promise not to tell you. Didn't want you to feel obligated since you know her. She thought you probably wouldn't like them but would be afraid to tell her."

"Let me handle it. I'll just tell her the truth. You and Reagan kept your promise and I found out on my own. No reason to make up a story. The truth is always the best. I need to pay her a visit anyway. I always come back feeling better about life after a visit with her."

"Did Reagan ask you about a place in the area to get some prints made from originals?"

"She did."

"She hoped you would think she was asking because she needed to print some of her originals, but two of Aunt Ida's watercolors have sold, and she wanted to make some prints before shipping the originals."

"I'll tell Reagan—"

"That's okay," Brett interrupted. "I'll tell her."

"What's going on between you two, Brett? Tell your old buddy."

"Nothing. She lives in Lonewild and I'm taking care of Lonewild."

"Sounds more like you're taking care of Reagan Hart."

"Don't go there. You know I have no intention—"

"Whatever you say. Okay. You tell Reagan, but let me tell Ida. I have a proposition for her. Let me run it by her, and if she's interested, I'll let you know."

"Sounds good, but be sure she knows I didn't spill the beans. I gotta run now, Dave. Leaving the office for an assignment at the capitol. Not too excited about it, but hey…it pays the rent."

"Sure. Didn't mean to keep you this long. I'll get back in touch after I talk with your aunt."

In a week and a half, Jared Loper had managed to build his business to twice the number of customers he started with by taking advantage of places that didn't mind putting his business cards on their checkout counters. Dog owners seemed especially glad to find someone to take over the task as the weather got colder, but Jared didn't mind cold weather. He'd always preferred winter to summer. Still a long way from being able to move out and find a place of his own, at least he was getting closer.

Just as he was getting dressed to do his first morning rounds, his phone rang and he looked down to see his dad's name pop up. They had been talking more regularly, and Jared felt relieved to be able to tell him each time that he'd added one or two more dogs to his routes.

"Hi, Dad."

"Good morning. I was wondering if you had plans for dinner tonight."

"Just pizza and beer with Al and Felix probably. Why?"

"Would you like to come over for my famous barbecued ribs? I could pick you up and take you back. There's someone I'd like you to meet."

"Sure. I could do that if it's after my afternoon rounds. Who is it?"

"You'll see when you get here. Let's just leave it at that."

"You're not going to tell me, are you?"

"No, I'm not," Henry said, "but at least you won't have to wait long to find out. Just a few hours. I'll see you at seven and text you when I'm five minutes away so you can meet me downstairs. Bye, son."

Jared leaned his head back against the chair and closed his eyes. The call hadn't taken him completely off guard. He'd suspected something was going on with his dad that might involve selling the house, but meeting someone new? That could mean only one thing. He drew in a deep breath and his mind began to race. He'd carried a photo of his mother in his wallet since his medical school days. He took it out and studied it. Donna Loper had been the one constant in his life. The only person who'd stood by him and believed in him no matter what.

The few times he'd gotten in trouble at school... When his dad had thought he needed to be punished... His mom always came to his rescue. If not by completely changing the scenario, at least by managing to lessen the punishment. The one time she tried and failed had netted him seven years in prison, and he suspected she never got over that. She'd developed breast cancer two years after his conviction and died after a three-year courageous battle with the disease.

It nearly killed him to see her after several rounds of chemotherapy. She was gaunt and frail and had lost her hair. She still visited him, but her visits always left him feeling worse. It was difficult to see her like that with a scarf tied around her hairless head.

He looked at the photo again and felt disgust. Not at himself for what his actions had done to her, but for what he suspected his dad was about to do to him. If his suspicion was correct, Jared was about to lose the one constant in his life that he still had. He could go back to his childhood home and visualize his mom in the kitchen, the vision conjuring up smells that he remembered to this day.

If his dad was going to try to take those memories away from him, his plan wouldn't be met with an agreeable son. No one could take the place of Donna Loper, and no house could replace his childhood home. Or…he could be totally off track, so he tried to put it out of his mind, picked up his coat, and walked out the door to start his morning rounds.

Referring to his dog walking as "rounds" was a bit sadistic, he thought. After all, to the original Jared the word "rounds" had some dignity. His patients looked up to him…almost as a god at times. He was the doctor who kept them from feeling pain during, and sometimes after, surgery. Why shouldn't they admire him? And admire him they did.

But to Jared 2.0, the word held a very different meaning. It almost stung. So why did he keep using it? Possibly as a form of self-punishment. A gentle cue to remind himself that things were much different now and would never be the same again. He could possibly find and maybe even re-establish his relationship with his daughter, but he was sure that Reagan would never forgive him and that they wouldn't be a family again. He could make a living walking dogs, but he would never be revered for his position as he once was. One of these days he would sleep in a bed again and have a closet for his clothes. That was his immediate goal. Finding his daughter could come either before or right after that, but Meredith was always in the forefront of his mind.

The text from Henry came through at exactly 6:55, and Jared slipped on his coat and called to Al, "I'm outta here!"

"Later, dude."

In the elevator he rehearsed what he would say if the news was indeed what he expected. Nothing sounded right. His dad certainly had the freedom to live his life the way he chose and with whom he chose. Jared knew that, but he had a foreboding feeling that this person Henry wanted him to meet was going to be yet another unwanted change in his life.

"Hello, son. I'm glad you were able to make it."

"Sure. Who was it you wanted me to meet?"

"Hold your horses. She's waiting at the house. Her name's Carole, and she's pretty important to me so I hope you like her, but there's no reason why you shouldn't."

The news that it was a woman didn't take Jared by surprise, but it was unwanted and unwelcome. "Why would it matter whether I like her?"

"Carole and I have been spending some time together, and I imagine the three of us will be too. She's very nice. I'm not saying there's anything permanent here. I just hope Carole and you and I can get together occasionally and enjoy each other's company, and I'm asking you to get to know her before you pass judgment."

"How long have you known her and where did you meet her?"

"Fair questions. We've been casual friends for a couple of years. Since she joined the faculty at the university. We started seeing each other socially about six months ago. First it was only with other faculty members in group settings. Then we started going to dinner together. Then a couple of Broadway plays and the symphony. We have similar interests so conversation comes easily. She has a couple of adult children, but they both live in California, so she doesn't see them often."

"How much does she know?"

"Everything."

"Great," Jared muttered sarcastically.

"Relationships are built on truth and trust, son. Not lies and deceit. She doesn't judge. That's not her style. She's eager to get to know you."

Jared bristled. "Why? Does she want to reform me?"

"Why would you ask a question like that?"

"Sorry. I just don't know how to navigate this new after-prison existence. It's hard to know who to trust. Hard to anticipate what people are going to think when they find out."

"It sounds like you're the one who's not giving *her* a chance before you even meet her. She's putting the finishing touches on the meal. Will you be pleasant and give her a chance? That's all I ask."

So she had already appropriated Donna Loper's domain. Could this news get any better? "Sure," Jared conceded. "It's not going to be easy seeing someone else in Mom's kitchen, though."

"Of course. I get that, but Mom's been gone for two years now, and that's a big, empty house I come home to every day. I'm starting a new chapter in my life just like you are. Speaking of… How's your business going?" Henry's abrupt change of subject wasn't lost on Jared, but he was ready for it. It wasn't easy to discuss a woman who apparently was trying to take his mom's place in his dad's life…and in Jared's childhood home.

"Keeps me busy. Getting new customers almost daily. It's building up more quickly than I thought it would."

"That's great news. I suspect you've found a niche that was just waiting to be filled and that your business will continue to grow. I'm proud of you for being proactive and going after this wholeheartedly."

"I hope so. We'll see. If it keeps growing like it has been, I guess I could hire a college kid to help with a few of them."

"There's that entrepreneurial spirit. Keep up the good work," Henry said as he pulled the car into the driveway. "Here we are."

"Yeah. Here we are."

"Carole, this is my son Jared. Jared, Dr. Carole Barlow."

"I'm glad to finally meet you, Jared."

"Dr. Barlow."

"Oh, goodness. Carole, please. I shed that cumbersome title as soon as I walk out of the door of the university."

Jared had never thought of the word "doctor" as a cumbersome title. It was one he'd worked long and hard for, and he'd been happy to have it as a part of his name. It seemed strange not to have it now, and yet here was a woman who didn't encourage its use where she was concerned. It just did not compute for him.

Carole continued the conversation. "I hear you have a thriving dog-walking business. That's wonderful. I'm a dog lover. I've had my present fur baby for four years now and he's the light of my life. I hire a walker for him during the middle of the day when classes preclude my going home for lunch."

"What breed is he?" Jared asked, relieved to have something to talk about besides his past.

"He's a rescue so I'm really not sure. The veterinarian says a poodle mix, maybe with some Maltese or Havanese. I could order a DNA test for around a hundred dollars to know for sure, but who cares really? I wouldn't love him any differently if I knew, you know?"

"Sure. I walk several poodles and poodle mixes. They're good dogs."

Henry broke in. "Food's on the table. Anyone hungry?"

"The ribs smell awesome, Dad."

"Carole made the carrot soufflé and broccoli slaw."

Jared realized he'd let his guard down. Carole was good at worming her way into a person's interests. He'd have to admit that. Was that how she'd strolled effortlessly into his dad's life? Found out what he was interested in and started talking about that? Jared could just imagine it.

Henry, I hear you like the symphony. So do I. And Broadway plays. What have you seen lately? I've been wanting to see so-and-so. Have you seen it?

Whatever she had done, she had apparently done it well... because from the look of it, it was working. His dad seemed pretty far gone. She was definitely attractive. Well-dressed. Well-spoken. What was not to like?

She wasn't Donna. That's what.

Chapter Fifteen

"Good morning, Ida," David said as he entered Sundown Assisted Living Center and saw Ida Carter sitting close to the front door.

"Is that David Norsworthy's voice I hear? Come closer so I can see you better. These old eyes, you know. Pull up that chair over there."

David bent over to give her a hug before he sat down. "How are they treating you here? It's such a lovely place. Are you getting three good meals a day?"

"The food's just okay. Nothing to write home about. Well, I guess this *is* home now, isn't it?" And there was that hearty Ida Carter laugh again. "They don't use salt, you know. Not good for us old folks, they think. I have to ask for the saltshaker at every meal. You'd think they'd know by now and bring it without my asking. I'm not complaining, though. I'd never complain about a place that took me in when I could no longer live alone."

"That's one of the main things I have always admired about you, Ida. I don't think I've ever heard you complain about anything. And I guess I've known you most of my life." David leaned forward in his chair and clasped her hand in his. "Do you remember when you used to babysit me? I was about five or six and Mom would bring me, and sometimes Nathan, to your house for the afternoon so she could go shopping in peace. I remember how much I loved going to Lonewild and rummaging around in that room upstairs you called your junk room. To us it was filled with all sorts of treasures. I realized later that most of those things were there for Brett, but I didn't know him then. I don't think I actually met him until he moved to Wentworth Cove after his parents were killed."

"That was a hard time for all of us. Such a tragedy. But I'm thankful Frank and Elaine and I were here for him. And he was a blessing to us. *Most* of the time anyway." She laughed. "I remember Elaine having to go up to the school a few times to talk with a teacher about something he'd done. Fortunately, they had the parent duties, and I got to sit back and act like the grandparent. I never had children of my own, of course, but I've come to realize that's the easier role. Spoil 'em and send 'em back to the parents."

"I guess that's right. Maybe I'll get to experience that one of these days. Jess is in college now."

"That's what I heard. Such a lovely girl. And is she still dating—is that what they call it these days—Bettie Grayson's grandson?"

"As far as I know, but she doesn't talk about him much. Elizabeth would be able to tell you more. I'm pretty sure they text every day."

"Text. That's something I never could understand. Like writing a letter without having to use postage or wait for it to be delivered. A good thing, I guess, but it's for the young folks. Give me a good old handwritten letter any day. Although I would have to get someone to read it to me now." That laugh again. The reason David enjoyed his visits with Ida. Her attitude was always upbeat and infectious.

"Ida, I came to see you today to hear that wonderful laugh. But there's another reason."

"Yes? Pray tell what could it be? Surely you don't want permission to dig around in my junk room again. I couldn't give it to you anyway. That lovely young lady and her precious—and precocious, I might add—daughter are living there now…thanks to you."

"It seems you've been keeping a secret from your old buddy David. I had no idea you were a painter."

"Oh, Lordy. Did that rascal Brett tell you? I told him…"

"No, Brett didn't tell me."

"Reagan? I thought I could trust—"

"Reagan didn't tell me either. In fact, she doesn't even know that I know. I was looking at her website to find a print of something we had in the gallery a few months ago and saw them. You can imagine how surprised I was. Ida, they're really good. I can't imagine why you wouldn't want me to put some in the gallery."

"You're just saying that. I know they're not that good. I just painted for fun. It was a diversion for the last few years. That's all."

"Did I have to tell you I'd seen them? No. I could have kept that information to myself and you never would have known the difference. If I'd thought they weren't good, that's exactly what I would have done. But that's not the case. I can't imagine why you wouldn't want to share them with the world."

"I didn't want you to feel obligated or put you in an uncomfortable position."

"It's my choice to ask you if I could feature some in the gallery. I would be honored."

"You would? My paintings in your gallery? Are you sure?"

"In fact, what I would really like to do is have a one-woman show featuring your paintings…with you there as a special guest. What do you say?"

"Oh, I don't know, David—"

"In full disclosure, I'm not being entirely altruistic here. You know one-person shows are good for the gallery because they bring in people who might not come otherwise. In this case, I'm pretty sure the whole town will show up. Is there a soul in Wentworth Cove you don't know?"

"Has Nathan and Tracy's baby been born yet?" Ida asked with a twinkle in her eye.

"No. She's not due for another six weeks, I think."

"Then I don't suppose so."

This time David had to laugh at the octogenarian's quick wit. "So what do you say? Would you be willing to allow me to make you a world-renowned artist?"

"Well… let me think about it. This is all so strange. I never for one minute thought my little watercolors would be seen by anybody but me."

"Okay, but I'm going to check back with you in a week. You will seriously consider it?"

"What choice do I have? You'll hound me until I give you an answer. I remember how insistent you could be when you were younger and I don't suppose you've changed. Give my love to Elizabeth, will you?"

"Of course. See you soon."

As soon as he got in the car, David dialed Reagan's number. "You won't believe who I've just seen and what we've been discussing."

"You're not even going to give me a hint?"

"It has to do with your landlady and her watercolors. How's that for a hint?"

"David! How did you find out? Did Brett—"

"Nobody told me. I made the discovery quite by accident. I was looking for a specific print on your website, and—"

"That possibility never crossed by mind. Was she upset?"

"Not at all. In fact, she's thinking about letting me feature her in a one-woman show."

"She's *what?*"

"You heard me."

"Does Brett know?"

"He knows I discovered the paintings but not that I've already talked with her. I think he'll be surprised that she's even considering it."

"He will indeed. Listen, David. I hate to cut this short, but I need to leave for the bookstore. Can I talk to you later about it?"

"Of course. I lost track of time this morning."

Reagan downed the last of her coffee and slipped on her coat. She was stunned that Ida Carter might allow her paintings to be shown at David's gallery. It was the last thing she expected to hear, but the news made her happy. Beauty should be shared with the world, and Ida's watercolors were things of beauty. She needed to get in high gear and have prints made of all the originals. From what she had heard about her landlady, most of the town would turn out...and who wouldn't want one of their beloved Miss Carter's masterpieces?

Chapter Sixteen

Dawn arrived misty and gray on Thursday in New York City, and by eight o'clock not much had changed as Jared was getting dressed for his morning rounds. Felix, as usual, lay on a blanket on the floor at the end of the couch that served as Jared's bed. The dog hadn't completely rejected his former master, but Jared was quickly becoming his favorite.

If Jared didn't take him out, Felix would lie at the door with his nose almost touching it waiting for his new master to return. Al didn't seem to care. He rarely came out of his bedroom anyway and was glad he no longer had to walk a dog. He would emerge just long enough to eat or watch college football with Jared occasionally.

"I'm heading out, Al," Jared called as he opened the door.

"Yeah. I've found something I think you'll be interested in, but I'll tell you about it when you get back."

"If it's about Reagan, I'll wait. I can walk the first group a little later."

"No. Let me see what else I can find while you're gone."

Memories of his life with Reagan and Meredith flooded Jared's mind as he walked his two morning groups of dogs. They'd been good years. His anesthesiology practice brought in enough money that Reagan didn't have to work and could stay home and take care of their child, born eleven months after the wedding.

Reagan was young when they married, but she'd been a good mother to Meredith. A good wife too. He'd often wondered why he thought he needed more money to take care of them. But in those rare times when he was being completely honest with himself, he had to admit the extra cash he made by selling opioid prescriptions was more for himself—his ego—than his family. Living in New York City was expensive, and he wanted a large, fancy apartment, nice clothes, and enough funds to be able to take expensive vacations every year.

Well...he'd earned himself a seven-year "vacation" he hadn't counted on. Who'd have thought one of his customers would take an overdose? And that others would testify against him at the trial? Those two possibilities had never entered his mind. If they had, of course he would've quit. But he thought himself untouchable and almost immortal. Many of his patients saw him as godlike when he was able to turn their post-surgical painful existence into a pain-free life. That adulation meant almost as much to him as the extra money.

The seven plus years in prison hadn't been a cakewalk, but they paled in comparison to what he'd lost. He hadn't really expected Reagan to stick around after she found out what he'd done. She'd always had a heightened sense of right and wrong. But he hadn't expected her to remove his only child from his life. Legally, she had every right to pack up and move away, but it was wrong and he must throw all of his effort into restoring his relationship with his daughter.

But Al had said he'd found something, and that thought made him walk a little faster.

Reagan still couldn't believe her landlady had so readily agreed to let David make her a featured guest at a reception and introduce her to the public as a watercolorist. In anticipation of a large crowd, Reagan and David had decided to make it an event to remember. Brett offered to help as much as his job would allow, so David assigned the publicity to him.

Brett knew Isaac Weiler, owner and editor of Wentworth Cove's weekly newspaper, but hadn't seen him in a couple of years. That would be a good place to start. Then post some fliers around town. And social media. Brett was kind of old school for his age when it came to the internet, but he did have a couple of social media accounts because his editor expected it. This would mean a lot to his aunt, and he was going to do everything in his power to make it a success.

Picking up his phone from his paper-scattered desk, he dialed Isaac's office.

"Wentworth Cove Courier, Isaac Weiler speaking."

"Isaac. Brett Mason here."

"Mason, my boy. How's everything going at the capital?"

"Busy as usual. How about you? You doing okay?"

"Slowing down here," Isaac said, leaning back in his chair. "I don't seem to have as much get-up-and-go as I did at your age. Imagine that."

"I'm sure you're still doing a great job with the paper, though. I was wondering if you could do me a favor."

"Name it and claim it."

Brett spelled out his request and offered to write it up and send it via email. Isaac agreed to run the write-up for the two weeks leading up to the event.

"I'll tell Miriam too. I know she'll want to get the Chamber of Commerce involved."

"Great. That's something I hadn't thought of."

"And Mason…"

"Yes?"

"Stop by the office next time you're out our way."

"I'll do that. I'd love to catch up over a cup of coffee."

"You buying?"

"You got it."

"It's a deal. My doc took me off caffeine, but what he doesn't know won't hurt him."

"What about decaf?"

"Oh heck, boy. Might as well have a cup of hot water with brown food coloring."

Brett signed off with Isaac, set his phone on his desk, and picked it up again. He should call Reagan and coordinate some of the publicity. Wasn't she helping David plan this event? Maybe she had some ideas. *Don't kid yourself, Mason. You know exactly what you're doing, and you know exactly why you're doing it. Maybe you need to take a step back.*

But his desire to hear her voice overruled his self-talk, and he dialed her number.

"Hi, Brett."

"Hey. I was thinking. David put me in charge of publicity for Aunt Ida's coming-out party, and I was wondering if you have any ideas. I've already talked to Isaac at the paper, and his wife will get the Chamber of Commerce involved. I'll do something with social media. Can you think of anything else?"

"What about putting up some posters in storefront windows?"

"Great idea. You volunteering to make them? Could I entice you with another meal?"

"Well, I never got that surf and turf."

This was going better than he'd expected. "There's a great place in Kennebunkport."

"Just kidding. I'd be happy to. Actually, what about Meredith? She loves to make posters and is a good little artist…if I do say so myself about my own daughter."

"I trust your judgment on that. Do you want to mention it to her, or do you want me to?"

"Why don't you do it? She still talks about how nice you were to move her furniture upstairs."

"Does she now? I have an admirer at Lonewild. Sweet!"

"You definitely have an admirer at Lonewild."

Just one? The thought had flitted across Brett's mind before he could stop it. Reagan's statement brought an interesting and unexpected sensation. A somewhat restrained excitement. No doubt she was talking about Meredith only.

Regaining his composure, he said, "When should I ask her?"

"We'll be home around four o'clock. Why don't you call her after that? I'll text you her number."

"I forget kids these days have their own phones. Will do."

"Yeah. I probably would have waited to get her one, but I want her to have it for safety reasons."

"Sure. I'll call her this evening. Gotta run and take care of my *real* job—the one that buys you meals for all you do for Aunt Ida. I guess Meredith will have to be in on the next one."

"I'm sure she'd love that," Reagan said.

Chapter Seventeen

Flinging open the door and kicking off his boots, Jared called to Al, who was still in his room with the door closed. "Hey, buddy. I'm back and ready to hear what you've found."

"Be there in a few. Wanna put one of those frozen meals in the microwave for me?"

"Sure."

When the microwave beeped, Al opened his door. "I think I might've stumbled on a gold mine. Well, I really didn't stumble. I did a little research. It might be nothing, but it's worth a look. You game?"

"That was a rhetorical question, right?"

"Yeah, I guess it was."

"What'd you find?"

"Remember that other person who had a few paintings on Reagan Loper's website? Ida Carter?" Al asked, digging in to his meatloaf and mashed potatoes.

"Vaguely. Why?"

"I googled her name and lo and behold, guess what I found in her local newspaper."

"I don't have time for guessing games, Al. Just tell me," Jared said, raising his voice.

"Whoa, buddy. Settle down. I *am* telling you. Remember, I'm the one doing this research. You might be a little bit appreciative."

"I am. I am. I just had to wait all afternoon, and I guess I'm a little on edge." Jared pulled out a chair and sat down.

"Anyway… Ida Carter lives in…drumroll, please…a little coastal village in Maine called Wentworth Cove. Found that out because the local newspaper had an article about her eighty-fifth birthday party a couple of years ago."

"So?"

"So…there's an art gallery in Wentworth Cove that's hosting a one-woman show for her in a couple of weeks. "

"And?" Jared asked, shrugging.

"And…put two and two together, man. If this is the right Reagan Loper, and if Ida Carter's work is on her website, and if there's a one-woman show at an art gallery in Wentworth Cove, Maine… Doesn't it stand to reason that Reagan would be there? Heck, she might even live there."

"That's a lot of *if*s."

"You're not going to have anything but *if*s until you know something for sure, and you're not going to know anything for sure unless you check it out. Or am I going to have to do that for you too?"

"What do you think I should do? Did you notice that I don't have a nice, shiny new set of wheels? And did you forget I can't leave the state?"

"Ever heard of a car rental? Ever heard of putting it in someone else's name?"

"Well… It would be risky, but I guess I'm going to have to take some risks," Jared said, and a new resolve seemed to take hold. "Where is Whatchamacallit Cove, Maine?"

"Wentworth. Think Kennebunkport and you've got it. It's about a five-hour drive from here."

"You figured all this out, and you don't even know if that's the right Reagan?"

"Bud, if you don't take a chance, you never will find her."

"You're right. I guess I'll have to do something with this information."

"Weren't you about to pick up a few more dogs and hire a college kid to help? Why not do that and let him sub for you for a couple of days? Just long enough to find out if it's really her. Wouldn't it be a hoot if it was and you showed up at that art gallery?" Al threw his head back and laughed. He seemed to be getting more pleasure out of this than Jared.

The thought of locating Reagan and Meredith was one thing. Actually confronting them was quite another. Jared hadn't stared that possibility in the face until now, and he wasn't sure how he felt about it. Why would he have conflicting feelings when that's what he'd wanted since his release from prison?

The—what were they calling it?—one-woman show was on a Sunday afternoon, and he didn't have as many dogs to walk on the weekend. It just might work. He could actually drive up there and back on the same day.

What would he say to her, though? If he caused a scene, there's no way she would let him see Meredith. He'd have to play it cool. Maybe a disguise would be best. Just until he knew for sure.

He thought about sharing his plan with Henry, but he knew what his dad would say. *Leave her alone, son. Give her some time.*

Maybe he should. But on the other hand, this could be his only chance, and he felt he had to take it.

"Meredith? This is Brett Mason."

Meredith sat down on the edge of her bed. "Hi, Mr. Mason. Mom said you were going to call, so I put your name in my phone as a contact."

"Don't you think someone who moved your bedroom furniture upstairs deserves to be called by his first name? 'Mr. Mason' is polite, but 'Brett' makes me think we're friends."

"Sure. If you don't mind."

"Only a friend would ask a favor like this. I heard you're a super poster maker and wondered if you'd be willing to make a few posters to advertise Aunt Ida's one-woman show at David's gallery."

"I'd love to!" Meredith jumped up and ran over to the corner of her room where her art supplies were stored. "And I have all the poster board and paint I'd need. Poster making is one of my favorite things!"

"I don't want it to take time away from your schoolwork."

"Could I do it over the weekend? We don't have homework then."

"Sure. That would be fine. I'd really appreciate it. And I'd love to take you and your mom to Kennebunkport for dinner sometime for all you're doing for Aunt Ida."

"I'm the one who discovered her watercolors, you know."

"So I heard." Brett smiled.

"She's really talented, and I like her a lot."

"She likes you too. Thanks for going to see her."

"I would go more often, but I have to wait until Mom can take me."

"If you'd like, I'll swing by and pick you up the next time I'm going," Brett offered. "That is, if it's okay with your mom."

"Oh, she won't mind."

"It's a deal then. How about I text you the details we need on the posters? You can decorate any way you think best. They're going to be displayed in windows of stores and businesses in Wentworth Cove."

"How many?"

"I'm sure I can find places for as many as you can do. Let's start with ten, though. Would you have time for that many?"

"Absolutely. No problem."

Chapter Eighteen

Jared Loper's alarm sounded at 5:00 AM on Sunday. He threw on the clothes he'd decided on the night before and a Red Sox cap, downed a quick cup of coffee and a breakfast bar, and took the elevator to the building garage. Opening the door to the car he'd rented in Al's name, he hesitated for a couple of seconds, weighing the risks against the possible gains.

He'd seen his parole officer on Friday and wouldn't have to check in for another couple of weeks, so that wouldn't be a problem. The car couldn't be traced to him, so that wouldn't be a problem. He'd hired and trained a college student to help with the dog walking, so that wouldn't be a problem. He'd have to drive slowly and carefully, though, because if he was caught out-of-state, the repercussions were huge. Likely, he'd be sent back to prison. That was the risk, but the gain was the possibility, the probability, of finding his daughter. All the evidence pointed to it, and for Jared that gain outweighed all the risks.

Decked out in her newest and brightest outfit, a coral pantsuit with a coral and lime green scarf, Ida Carter emitted a queenly air as she sat in a brown leather wingback chair in Norsworthy Art Gallery. Though hesitant at first, she'd come around and even warmed to the thought of being the center of attention, along with her paintings. As people from Wentworth Cove and a few from towns nearby greeted her and oohed and aahed over her watercolors, she feigned surprise that so many people had shown up for her "coming out party," as she called it.

Though she couldn't see well enough to identify some of the people, Elizabeth told her who they were, and she pretended to have known all along. David was busy ringing up sales, and Reagan and Brett made sure the food and drinks didn't run out. Meredith was hanging out with Daniel and a couple of other friends from school.

Brett spotted the man first and thought it strange that he was alone and seemed to be more interested in people-watching than looking at art. He also hadn't made an effort to speak to Ida, and didn't seem to know anyone else in attendance. "I think my journalist's sixth sense is kicking in, but I'm going to check out something. Be right back," he said to Reagan.

"Sure. I'm going to the kitchen to get more scones," she answered.

Brett walked toward the man with the Red Sox cap and stuck out his hand. "Hello. I'm Brett Mason, Ida Carter's nephew. I don't think I've met you."

"Mike Porter."

"Welcome, Mike. Would you like some refreshments? A drink?"

The man continued to look around instead of making eye contact with Brett. "No. I just came by to see the paintings."

You're not going to get off that easy. "Do you live around here?"

"In the area for a brief time."

"Let me introduce you to the artist." *If you're here for her special day, surely you'd like to meet her. If that's why you're really here...*

"She seems busy. I'll just look around," the man said.

Brett couldn't pinpoint anything worrisome, so he backed off. "Let us know if you have any questions," he said and returned to the refreshments table.

Jared spotted her from across the room as soon as she returned from the kitchen with a bag of scones. Although it had been seven plus years, he had no doubt it was Reagan. Her hair was a little longer and she'd added highlights, but other than that, she hadn't changed. And if Reagan was here, so was Meredith. He continued to scan the room.

"Did you learn anything from your journalistic investigation?" Reagan asked Brett as he helped her put the scones on a tray.

"See that guy over there?" he said.

"Which one?"

"The guy with the Red Sox cap."

At that moment their eyes met. He looked so different—but the way he held himself, the way he moved, the eyes, even behind glasses—she had no doubt.

Her fingers tightened around a scone, reducing it to crumbs. "I have to go," she whispered to Brett. "Could you get Meredith and tell her I have a headache? Don't bring her to Lonewild, though. I'll let you know where I am."

"What is it? What's going on?" Was he about to find out why Samantha said she seemed mysterious?

"Don't let him see you leave with her! Take her out the back door."

"Who is it, Reagan? The guy in the cap, right?"

"I'll tell you everything later. Just please help me!" Her voice had an urgency that told him this was a serious situation.

"Okay. Text me where you are, and I'll bring Meredith to you."

"Brett, wait." She ducked behind a large man and continued in a low voice. "Tell her 'Daisy's in the dollhouse.'"

"Huh?"

"'Daisy's in the dollhouse.' Say that to Mere so she'll know to go with you. Gotta run." She backed into the kitchen and flew out the back door to her car.

Brett sauntered over to Meredith as inconspicuously as possible. Out the corner of his eye he could see the man facing away from him and looking around on the other side of the room. "Hey, Mere. Can you help me in the kitchen a minute?"

"Sure. Back in a sec, Daniel."

"Listen. Your mom had to leave. Said she had a headache. Wants me to bring you to her. Said to tell you 'Daisy's in the dollhouse.'"

"That's our code if I ever need to go with a stranger, but you're not a stranger so I don't know why I needed the code."

"I guess she just wanted you to feel extra safe."

"Could I stay with the Parkers and let them bring me home? I know they wouldn't mind."

"Well, it's not up to me. I'm just doing what your mom wanted me to do."

"She left in that big of a hurry? There's only one reason… My dad! Did she see—?"

"I'm not sure. She just said she had a headache and had to leave. She's going to text me where to take you to meet her. Let me text David real quick. Why don't you go into the bathroom and lock the door? I'll knock twice when I'm ready."

"It's my dad. I know it is. He found us, didn't he?"

"I don't know anything about that, but I want to take care of you, and your mom trusted me to do that."

"I'll be in the bathroom. I'm gonna text Mom from there."

"See where she wants us to meet her."

Dave, something's going on with Reagan. She left because of a "headache" and wants me to bring Meredith to her, but not to Lonewild. There's a strange guy in a black Red Sox cap here milling around. Have you seen him? I think it has something to do with him.

I saw him. No idea who he is. Unless...

Unless what?

That's Reagan's story to tell.

Could you keep him distracted while I get Mere out of here?

Will do. Keep me posted.

Text Reagan and tell her we're on our way.

As soon as Brett saw David talking to "Mike," he knocked twice on the bathroom door. "Let's go."

"I'm not going," Meredith said when she was back in the kitchen.

"Why not?"

"If it's my dad, I want to see him. I'll go after that. I won't talk to him. I just want to see him first."

"I don't know who or what or why, but I'm doing what your mom asked me to do. She wants what's best for you. You know that."

139

"I want to see him first," she insisted.

"Please go with me to the car."

"All right... but you better be glad I like you."

"I am. Believe me. I am."

Brett managed to get Meredith in the car without being noticed. "Did you ask your mom where she is?"

"She said go to the library in Kennebunk. What did he look like? Brett, please tell me."

"You know what, Meredith. I'm going to let you ask your mom those questions. I don't know anything about the situation, so I don't want to do or say something she wouldn't want."

"You like her, don't you?"

"Your mom? Of course, I do."

"I mean you like, 'like' her," Meredith persisted.

"Is that your generation's way of saying 'in a romantic sense'?"

"I guess."

"Well, Mere. Let me put it this way. Your mom is smart and sweet and talented...and did I mention very attractive? What's not to like?"

"I knew it!" Meredith exclaimed. "You should tell her. You should ask her out. On a real date, I mean. Not just because she helped with the show."

"You don't beat around the bush, do you?"

"Did you know she hasn't been on a date since she divorced my dad seven years ago?"

"I'm not sure she'd go. She hasn't given me any reason to think she would."

"She's forgotten how to flirt. Besides, she's had a lot of things to think about since we decided to leave New York... I'm sorry. I forgot to text Mrs. Parker and ask her to tell Daniel and Molly I had to leave early."

Brett's phone rang as they were pulling into the parking lot at Kennebunk Public Library. "Yeah, David?"

"You need to get here as soon as possible. Your aunt collapsed. I think she's had a heart attack. Elizabeth said she didn't feel well, grabbed at her chest, tried to get out of the chair, and then just slowly crumpled to the floor."

"Is she—"

"She's alive," David assured him. "The paramedics are on their way. And Brett... You won't believe this. As soon as it happened that guy who calls himself Mike rushed over, told everyone to back away, yelled 'Call 911. Tell them to bring morphine and GTN,' and started giving her CPR. Then he said, 'Someone give me a non-coated aspirin...STAT!'"

"Wha—"

"Yeah. You might want to tell Reagan. Might mean something to her."

"What's going on here, David? Never mind. I don't have time. I need to be with Aunt Ida now. Should I meet them at the hospital?"

"That might be best. Where are you?"

"Kennebunk. Dropping off Meredith at the library as soon as I'm sure Reagan's here."

"Kennebunk Regional is where they'll take her. I hear the siren now. Why don't you head that way, and you can meet them at the ER."

"Call me if—"

"I will. The Parkers have formed a prayer circle in the kitchen. Elizabeth's going to ride in the ambulance with her. I'll follow in the car."

"I'll leave as soon as I get Meredith to her mom," Brett said and put his phone down on the console.

"I could hear David, you know," Meredith said. "My dad saved your aunt's life, didn't he?"

"That's a lot of conjecture, but Aunt Ida had what they presume is a heart attack, and someone we don't know rushed over and started doing CPR."

"My dad's a doctor," Meredith said matter-of-factly.

Brett let that sink in as he went around and opened the car door for Meredith. "Let's go in and find your mom," he said, putting his arm around her shoulder and feeling a sudden need to protect her. "Then I have to get to the hospital."

Trying to find the words to convey what had happened without further alarming Reagan, Brett explained the situation as best he could when they entered the library and located her behind some shelves.

"If you're worried he'll find you, you and Meredith need to get someplace safe. I think Lonewild is perfect, but if you're not comfortable staying alone, why don't you stay with David and Elizabeth until you have time to further assess the situation?"

"We'll be fine at Lonewild. The only thing I worry about now is that he apparently knows we live here in Maine. But, Brett. You need to go. Go to the hospital. And please keep us updated about Ida."

"Will do. I'll check on you later. Keep your phone charged."

"Did you see him at the gallery, Mom?" Meredith asked when they were alone. "I wanted to, but Brett wouldn't let me."

"Brett was just doing what I asked him to do. So if you're going to blame anyone, you can blame me."

"What did he look like? Same as the last time you saw him?"

"He tried to disguise himself, but I could tell. I don't know how he found us, but we have to be doubly careful now."

"I think Dad saved Miss Carter's life."

"That's a possibility. I just can't believe all this happened at an event that was supposed to be fun for her."

"I guess in a way it's a good thing he found us, isn't it? I mean if he really did save her life…"

"It's complicated. For one thing, he wasn't supposed to leave New York State. He could go back to prison for that if his parole officer finds out. That's one reason we moved to Maine and not upstate New York."

"You're not going to tell his parole officer, are you?"

"Today changes everything, Mere. I don't know what I'm going to do. I don't want to be looking over my shoulder every minute of every day."

A text from Brett popped up.

She's alive and stable. I'll see her in a few minutes when she gets to a room. The guy who did CPR disappeared, though. People tried to find him to thank him, but he'd vanished in all the hubbub while the paramedics were getting her into the ambulance. How are you and Mere?

Still at the library but heading to Lonewild in a minute.

I'll stop by after I'm sure Aunt Ida's settled in and resting.

I don't know...

I'll be careful. If I have even the slightest idea someone is following me, I'll pull in to the police station.

Okay. If you're sure you have time.

I'm staying with David and Elizabeth tonight. Already told my editor I won't be in tomorrow. And I might stay until Aunt Ida's out of the hospital. I can work remotely for a few days.

Reagan and Meredith had been home for about an hour when Brett's text popped up on both of their phones.

I'm at the kitchen door. No one followed me.

Meredith was the first to get to the door. "Brett," she said with emotion in her voice, "will you please persuade Mom not to tell his parole officer?"

"Come in, Brett. Mere, don't try to get him mixed up in this. It's our situation to deal with." Reagan's stomach was in knots and her heart was pounding in her chest. The nightmare had begun as soon as she'd heard about Jared's early release from prison, but now she was awake, and it was no longer a dream.

"Well, you asked him to take me to the library…so I guess you're the one who got him involved already. And Dad did save his aunt's life, so I think he should have an opinion."

Brett laughed. "Harvard Law School will be recruiting you any minute now." He pulled Meredith into a quick side hug and turned to Reagan. "I just came by to make sure you two were okay."

"Do you have time for coffee?" Reagan asked. "I think you deserve to know the whole story. After all, as Meredith said, I did get you involved in this."

She'd thought about telling him numerous times, but the opportune moment hadn't presented itself. Now, she thought, was as good a time as any…and he did deserve to know. Although they hadn't known him as long as they'd known David and Elizabeth, he'd become a trusted friend. The first person she'd turned to when she needed to get Meredith away from the gallery.

Meredith's phone rang in her jeans pocket. "It's Daniel, Mom. He's calling from home. Is it okay if I call him back? What should I tell him about why I left so fast?"

"'Oh, what a tangled web we weave' comes to mind. Tell him I'll explain everything to his mom soon. Tell him Miss Carter's doing well now."

"Okay. I'm going upstairs. Let me know if you need any help persuading her, Brett."

"I don't know about that one," Reagan said as soon as Meredith had left the room. "Sometimes I think she's too smart for her own good. But before I tell you about Jared… How's Ida. Did she have a heart attack? What's the prognosis and how long will she have to stay in the hospital?"

"She's resting. And yes, it was a heart attack. They're keeping her overnight and running some more tests tomorrow. Reagan…the emergency room doctor said the guy who performed CPR saved her life. I don't know who he is, but he apparently reacted instinctively and did what needed to be done until the paramedics arrived. Then he just vanished. I heard that a couple of guys tried to find him but couldn't."

"My ex-husband was a doctor."

"Meredith told me."

"Did she tell you he was in prison for seven years?"

Brett's eyes widened, and Reagan could tell by his expression that was the first time he'd heard about Jared's sullied past.

"I'm giving you an exclusive here, but it's for your ears only." Brett nodded, and she relayed the story as quickly as she could, trying not to leave out any pertinent information, but also feeling the need to protect their privacy somewhat.

"What an ordeal you've been through. And this whole time you were afraid he'd try to see Meredith…for what purpose? Did you think he'd kidnap her? Or try to get custody?"

"Both of those were possibilities, in my mind at least, but the most important reason was that I didn't want Meredith to be influenced by someone who valued the lives of other people so little. Someone whose career was based on the Hippocratic Oath to do no harm. He gave it all away because of greed. Gave his career away. Gave us away." Reagan could feel her chest tightening and realized her hands had formed into fists, so she got up and started busying herself with dishes. "Maybe he didn't think about the consequences, but he *should* have. And during the trial, his attitude was so cavalier toward the people whose lives were ruined by his disregard for their wellbeing." She turned toward the sink and hoped Brett hadn't seen her brush a tear off her cheek.

"You realize since he was in prison in New York State that he just violated parole, right?"

"I do."

"And you're sure it was him?"

She composed herself and sat back down. "I am. I mean, he'd disguised himself pretty well, but I'd know those eyes anywhere, even behind glasses, which he never wore before. He cut his hair and grew a beard. Which tells me he wasn't planning to out himself. I'm sure he knows he messed up by coming to Ida's rescue."

"He's probably sweating bullets right now."

Reagan's phone rang. "It's Elizabeth. I'll text her that we're okay and I'll call her back later."

Brett took a sip of coffee while Reagan was texting and thought about whether he should get even more involved than he already was. He'd become quite fond of both Reagan and Meredith and cared what happened to both of them, but his life had been running pretty smoothly lately.

"So what are you going to do?" he asked when she'd dropped her phone back into her purse. "If you say anything to the authorities, you know they'll probably send him back to prison, right?"

"And if they did, I wouldn't have to worry about something like this happening again. I could relax for the first time since I heard he was getting out early."

"Have you considered what Meredith wants?"

"I left everything I've ever known and moved to this small town because of Meredith. Of course, I've considered her," she snapped. "I did this for her."

"All I know is that she begged me to let her see her dad before we left the gallery. I was lucky she decided to go with me. I was afraid she wasn't going to. She really wanted to see him. Reagan, it's curiosity now, but that curiosity could easily grow into resentment. And that resentment would be aimed at you."

"I don't trust him," Reagan said, her jaw clenched. "She's been a happy, well-adjusted girl for the seven years he's been in prison. We've been fine, the two of us. Why would I want to rock the boat now?"

"Because she's twelve years old now, not five. And she knows he risked his freedom when he rushed to Aunt Ida's aid. I don't know much about teenage girls, but I know human nature, and she's seeing him now as a hero."

"That's it for you, isn't it? He saved your aunt's life so you're giving him the benefit of the doubt. Did you forget I told you he was responsible for the death of someone he sold opioid prescriptions to? Did you know he took Mere with him on one of his deliveries?" Reagan's volume increased with each question.

Brett calmly held her gaze. "Of course I'm thankful, but I'm not thinking about me or even Aunt Ida here. I'm thinking about what this is going to do to Meredith. All I'm saying is…I think you should let her have a say in what you do. You're doing this for her, and she's a smart young lady. You can reason with her. Maybe you should give it some thought before you do something rash like calling his parole officer."

Although she was boiling over inside, Reagan was careful to keep her tone unemotional. "I'm tired, Brett. I, uh…I just need time to think. Do you mind?" He put his hand on hers, and she pulled hers away.

"I should go back to the hospital anyway," he said. "I'll check on you tomorrow?" It was a question. He wasn't sure how she felt, but he was beginning to suspect Reagan interpreted his concern as interference, and he would have to tread softly.

"I don't think so. You just take care of Ida. Meredith and I will be okay. We have to work this out for ourselves. I don't need anyone trying to influence her to give up everything we worked for with this move." And just like that she'd confirmed his suspicion.

"Reagan, I—"

"Why don't you go check on your aunt now? I need to call Emily Parker and Elizabeth."

Brett took a deep breath, rose slowly, put on his coat, and exited Lonewild through the kitchen door, not knowing when he would return. He'd apparently blown it with Reagan, but he felt firm in his resolve that Meredith deserved to be able to see her father. Not for her dad's sake, but for Meredith's…and ultimately Reagan's too.

Chapter Nineteen

As soon as Brett walked out the door, the tears came to Reagan like a cloudburst. But she couldn't decide if she was crying because Jared had found them or she'd just rejected the kindness of someone who'd come to mean more to her than she'd dared to admit to herself. Whichever it was, she was a bundle of emotions and felt an urgent need to call Ryan. *He'll be the voice of reason. Tell me what to do about Jared. How to deal with Mere. Calm me down.*

She rifled through her purse for her phone and punched in his number. "Ry?"

"Hey. I started to call you, but I thought you might still be busy at the gallery. How'd the event for your landlady go?"

Just as she was beginning to give her brother and play-by-play, Meredith walked in and she put the phone on speaker.

"Mere's here now, so she can jump in if I leave out anything."

When she got to the part about Ida's heart attack, Meredith did indeed jump in. "Uncle Ryan, Dad saved her life. He was in disguise but risked having his cover blown by giving her CPR."

"Did you see him, Meredith?" Ryan asked.

"No, but Mom did. I wanted to, but Brett wouldn't let me."

"Brett?"

"We told you about Brett. He's Miss Carter's nephew and takes care of Lonewild for her," Reagan explained.

"So he knows about everything? About Jared?" Ryan asked.

"He does now," Meredith said. "He thinks we shouldn't tell his parole officer and that I should be able to see him. Doesn't he, Mom?"

"Why is this guy even offering his opinion on the situation? You just met him. When? A couple of months ago?"

"I know that, but he's really nice…and he likes Mom."

"Meredith!" Reagan exclaimed. "Why would you say that?"

"Because he told me on the way to the library."

"He just came right out and told you that he likes your mom?" Ryan asked. "He like, 'likes' her…as you kids say these days?"

"Yep."

"Well, I doubt that…but if he did, I'm pretty sure he doesn't now," Reagan said. "I just showed him the door. I don't think he'll be back any time soon."

"Mom! Why did you do that?"

"Okay. Okay. Hold on, you two," Ryan broke in. "Let's table this discussion for a minute and get back to the original reason for the call. What are you going to do, Rea? About Jared."

"What do you think I should do?"

"I think you have to see him. Talk to him. Let him know you have leverage. If he tries to do anything, you have the power to put him back in prison."

"And I can see him too, right?" Meredith continued to be relentless in her determination to see her father.

"Your mom needs to talk to him first. After that, she can decide if it's in your best interest to see him. I trust her to make the right decision. She's done a great job taking care of you all these years that she's had to do it alone."

"Brett's the only one on my side," Meredith complained, "and now he's gone. That's really not fair."

"You know I'm on your side. Always have been. Always will be. I just think your mom should take it slow and easy and see what the situation in New York is. Have you talked to Henry, Rea? Does he know about any of this?"

"No," Reagan answered, "but I thought about calling him. Do you think I should?"

"Can I at least see Grandpa?" Meredith begged her mom.

"Maybe. We'll see."

"I've missed him."

"We all have, Mere," Ryan said. "I can fly up and meet you in New York, Rea. Let me see what I can do, and I'll be back in touch."

After they'd hung up and Meredith had returned to her room, Reagan wasn't sure what to do next. Never in her life had she been faced with such a life-altering decision. If she didn't confront Jared, she'd always wonder when he'd show back up and what he would do. If she did confront him, what would she say? How would he react? She knew he could be hot-headed.

How could she best handle the situation? Did she have enough leverage to intimidate him into leaving them alone? She knew now the kind of man he was—one who wasn't afraid of taking risks to get what he wanted—and she was sure he wouldn't stop until he saw his daughter.

His daughter. She was, after all. But did that give him the right to have a relationship with her? Or had he relinquished his rights to fatherhood when he'd made a choice to put her at risk by taking her with him on one of his illegal prescription sales outings? Reagan knew she had some heavy decisions to make—and those decisions would affect the rest of their lives. She needed closure on the Jared issue. Could she be strong and persuasive enough to rein in her ex-husband?

Wentworth Cove was all abuzz about the mysterious stranger who'd breezed into town, shown up at a community art event, saved Miss Ida Carter's life, and vanished into thin air. Who was he? Where'd he come from? Where'd he go? Did anyone know him? How'd he know exactly what to do until the paramedics arrived?

Isaac Weiler's *Wentworth Cove Courier* carried the story of Miss Carter's show at Norsworthy Art Gallery, along with photos Josh Whitehall of *The Maine Way* magazine had taken and donated. One photo especially intrigued the editor. A full-on close-up of the Cove's newest hero.

Isaac had always loved a good mystery, and this seemed to be the mystery of the century in this little village. If he could identify the man, interview him, and write an article about him…well, he mused, it might just go viral. And wouldn't that be good publicity for the *Courier*. Impatient to get moving on his idea, he dialed Brett's number. As good a place to start as any, he thought.

"Mason, my man. How's your aunt this morning?" he asked, not wanting to seem as though he was only after a hot story.

"She's stable," Brett answered. "Resting well. I'm here with her now, but they're going to get her in a few minutes to run some more tests. It appears she might need a stent. There's apparently some blockage."

"So sorry to hear that. Amazing what they can do these days, though. Give her my best wishes for a speedy recovery."

"I will."

"You weren't at the gallery when she collapsed, were you?" Isaac asked.

"No. Something had come up, but I was planning to come back before everybody left."

"So do you know who this mysterious guy is? Or where he went? Or why he left so suddenly?"

"Not really." *Be careful here, Mason. Isaac's a good sleuth.* "Just that he told me his name was Mike Porter. But that's all the information I got out of him…and that was before all the commotion."

"You planning to stay at the hospital all day?"

"No, I'm going back to David's to work on some *Trib* stuff. Told my editor I'd get a couple of articles to him by tonight. I'll check on Aunt Ida again this afternoon. She's starting some in-home rehab."

"Can you spare a few minutes for that coffee we talked about?"

"I think so. You talking about this morning?"

"Whenever you can make it."

"I could meet you at the diner in about thirty."

"Thirty. Easy for a journalist to remember, eh? Only a journalistic dinosaur would think of something like that, I guess. That's what I am now, you know."

"You're one of a kind, Isaac. You've always been my role model. I'll never forget the day you came to our senior English class to talk about journalism as a career."

"Well, I inspired a good one. You've made quite a name for yourself over there in the capital city. And unlike what "thirty" represents in journalistic circles, I kind of hope this meeting signals a beginning, not an ending. I'll just let you speculate about that until I see you at Down East…in thirty."

"You're a sly one. You've piqued my curiosity. See you then."

Isaac was being cryptic for a reason—to get Brett's imagination juices flowing. Because the offer he was about to hit him with would require a lot of consideration and perhaps some creative thinking.

All the way from the hospital to Down East Diner, Brett tried to imagine what Isaac possibly could have meant when he mentioned he wanted their meeting to signal a beginning of something. He didn't want his imagination to run wild, but he couldn't think of anything other than a job offer. However, The *Courier* was a small local paper, and Isaac had run it essentially by himself for years. He had a front office assistant who took care of ads and subscriptions and occasionally wrote an article or two, but that was it. Isaac and the *Courier* were one and the same— joined at the hip—and had been, at least since Brett had moved in with his grandparents.

The day was cold, but the sky was a brilliant blue and the clouds as white as cotton balls. Brett's drive took exactly fifteen minutes, and through the window he saw his friend sitting in a booth as he pulled into the parking lot at the diner. He was still in a quandary about the reason for the meeting as he slid into the booth across from Isaac.

"Have you been here long?" Brett asked.

"Nah. Just long enough to order coffee and a piece of coconut pie. What can Janie get for you?" Isaac asked, waving over the server. "My treat."

"Since I didn't take time for breakfast this morning, a piece of pie and coffee would suit me just fine. Hi, Janie," he said. "Do you still serve that apple pie that tastes like cinnamon?"

"You name it, we have it," she said. "Good to see you, Brett. I hear Ida's improving now. I miss seeing her. She used to come in a lot when she was still driving."

"She's doing much better today. I'm sure she'll be dancing out of that hospital in no time, right after she gets all those nurses and doctors straightened out."

"Glad to hear it. Give her my best. Pie and coffee coming right up."

When Janie had walked away, Brett turned his attention back to Isaac. "I can't for the life of me imagine what you wanted to talk about, but when you said you hope this meeting will be the beginning of something...well, that was quite a hook."

"I'm not getting any younger, Mason."

"You don't seem to be getting any older either."

"You're kind, but you're not a very good liar. Miriam's term as mayor is over in May, and she's not planning to run again."

"I'm sorry to hear that. She's been good for the Cove."

"Well, thanks. I think so too, but she's not getting any younger either. Don't tell her I said that," Isaac said, laughing. "We've been talking about doing some traveling while we still can. We've never been to Hawaii, and I want to see those hula girls while I can still appreciate them. And Miriam wants to go to Paris again. We went on our honeymoon—of course that was a hundred years ago— but she's always wanted to go back. We've been too busy raising kids and taking care of the *Courier* and the Cove to take care of ourselves. To do what we want to do while we're able."

"Sounds like a good plan."

"You know both of our girls are married with families and live in Chicago and...well, they don't have any desire to move back to Maine, even though they grew up here."

"I didn't know them well since they were a few years older."

"I have grandchildren in college," Isaac said, pulling out his wallet and showing a couple of photos. "Can you believe that?"

At this point Brett was beginning to wonder if Isaac was ever going to get around to the point of the meeting, and his mind was racing with wild ideas.

"I guess you're wondering what I wanted to talk to you about."

"Well, I—"

"I'll quit reminiscing and cut to the chase. I'm hanging up my visor, Brett, and I want you to consider taking over the *Courier.*"

"Taking it over? Wha—"

"I want you to run it and eventually own it. The girls don't want it. Miriam and I don't need what little money it would bring in if I sold it. I want you to have it."

"Isaac, I—"

The old editor cut in before Brett could object. "Let me finish. I know you're doing well in Augusta—and you might not even want to move back—but you're known and respected in this town. You're a darn good reporter, and the *Courier* needs young blood. It needs someone who can take a solid local paper and make it even better. It needs someone who knows how to run a news website. I believe you can do that."

Brett swallowed hard. "I, uh… I appreciate the confidence you have in me. And if you'd given me this opportunity, say…a couple of days ago, I'd probably have jumped at it. I've been thinking about what it would be like to live here again. Chasing politicians all over the state is tiring, and frankly, …I'm sick of dealing with the corruption. But things have changed for me recently. On one hand I need to be closer to Aunt Ida, but other things are…well, up in the air, you might say. I'm not sure it's in my best interest to live here right now."

"I don't want an answer now. I want you to mull it over for a while. Think of the pros and the cons. Make a list. See which side of the paper outweighs the other."

"It's certainly a generous—and unexpected—offer, and I will give it serious thought. When do you need to know?" Brett asked his old friend.

"As I said, Miriam's retiring when her term is up in May, but I'd like to bring you on board before that if you're interested. Get a feel for small-town living again while I'm still here. Say, after the first of the year?"

"Deal." Brett reached out his hand across the booth. "I'll let you know by Christmas."

Chapter Twenty

With much trepidation Reagan stepped off the plane, proceeded down the ramp, and entered JFK International. Ryan should arrive in less than an hour, so she'd have time to get a bite to eat while she waited. That is, if she *could* eat. Reagan hadn't felt much like eating since she'd made up her mind to confront Jared and remind him that she had the upper hand. If he would toe the line, stay in New York, and not try to contact his daughter, she wouldn't tell his parole officer about his little out-of-state jaunt.

She'd obtained Jared's phone number from Henry, and she and Ryan were planning to see her ex-father-in-law while they were in town. Although, she really didn't think of Henry as an ex. She'd always felt close to Jared's parents, and after Jared went to prison, she continued to visit them on a regular basis…as much for her sake as for Meredith's.

It was just Henry now, and when she'd called to get Jared's number, he was excited to hear from her. She felt guilty thinking he probably expected her to be ready to

158

forgive and forget, but she and Ryan were going to explain the situation to him as gently as possible. The last thing Reagan wanted to do was hurt the man who'd been like a father to her for thirteen years.

She took her taco basket to a booth and texted Ryan so he would know where to find her. They'd decided to bring only carry-ons to avoid baggage claim, and since they were flying the same airline, he shouldn't have any trouble locating her gate and the fast-food place she'd chosen near it.

During her hour in the air, Reagan had rehearsed what she would say to both Henry and Jared. Since she'd decided to confront her ex-husband, her mind had been swarming with possibilities. She knew Henry hadn't mentioned the call to Jared because she'd asked him not to and he'd always been trustworthy. He was as mad at Jared as she was when they first learned about the prescription sales. It was Donna who tried to soften both of them toward her son. She'd always taken up for him, and although his actions had repulsed her, he was still her son and she gave him the benefit of the doubt. He was probably sorry, she said. Surely he wouldn't have done it if he'd known it would cause a death. He was a doctor, after all.

He *was* a doctor, and that's what made it even more incredulous to Reagan. He was a grown man. No longer Donna's little boy. And he should have known better. She didn't know if she could ever forgive him for what he'd done...to his patients and to his family.

But now she had to deal with her daughter, *his* daughter, who was five when her father went to prison, and a very savvy twelve years old now. Meredith wasn't happy when she learned her mom was going to New York and she wasn't. Reagan had made arrangements for her to stay with David and Elizabeth, and now that Ida was doing better and Brett had gone back to Augusta, they had plenty of room.

Meredith's plea was based on the fact that her dad had put his freedom at risk when he'd left New York to see them, and again when he'd rushed to Miss Carter's aid with no apparent concern that it might blow his cover. She was convinced he was contrite…and she wanted a chance to get to know him.

It didn't help matters, Reagan thought, that Brett had agreed with Meredith, petitioning Reagan to let her daughter see her father. She was just curious now, he'd said, but that curiosity could turn into resentment if Reagan continued to keep them apart. And it would only make matters worse if she decided to inform his parole officer and have him sent back to prison. It hadn't been easy to distance herself from someone she was growing rather fond of, but Reagan couldn't let her growing feelings for Brett get in the way of protecting her daughter.

As she was mulling over her ambivalent feelings about her landlady's nephew, a text from Ryan popped up on her phone.

Deplaning now. See you soon.

Thankful Ryan had been able to join her in the city, Reagan wolfed down the rest of her second taco and finished off her drink. The sooner they were able to get to Henry's house, the better she would feel. He expected them in an hour, and it would take about that long, Reagan suspected, to rent a car and get there from the airport.

"Hey." Ryan kissed his sister on the cheek and slid into the booth across from her.

"I'm so glad you're here. Are you hungry?"

"No. I had some snacks on the plane. Let's get this show on the road." He grabbed both of their bags and ushered his sister to the AirTrain, which would transport them to the car rental company.

Henry welcomed both Reagan and Ryan with a bear hug as he swung the door open. "It's been too long!"

"Hello, Henry," Ryan responded. "We've missed you. All three of us. Meredith couldn't come with us on this trip, but I feel sure you'll get to see her soon." He glanced over at Reagan, who just smiled.

"I've missed my girls. You, too, Ryan."

"I hope this is a new beginning for us, Henry," Reagan responded, finding her voice. "I'll bring Meredith soon."

"Come into the kitchen. Do you mind sitting at the table?" Henry asked.

"It'll be like old times. Feels good to be here. Kind of like we never left," Reagan said. "We had some good times, good meals, in that kitchen."

"Let's go then. There's someone I want you both to meet."

Reagan's heart skipped a beat. She hadn't expected… "I didn't know you had company."

"Reagan. Ryan. This is Dr. Carole Barlow," Henry said, walking over and putting his arm around the lady who was standing in Donna's kitchen.

"Carole…please," she said.

"Carole, it's nice to meet you," Ryan said, extending his hand.

"Yes." Reagan followed her brother's lead.

"Henry has told me so much about you two that I feel as though I know you already," Carole said. "Can I get you something to drink? Coffee? Mulled cider?"

"Cider sounds wonderful," Ryan replied. "Thanks."

"Nothing for me," Reagan said, as she took a couple of steps toward the door. "Henry, I wanted to talk to you in private. I didn't know you would have company. We should come back tomorrow."

"Carole is very special to me," Henry started, "and she knows about the whole situation. Anything you can say to me, you can say in her presence."

"It's not a pleasant topic, and I'd really rather speak to you alone."

"Reagan, I've asked Carole to marry me, and she's accepted." Henry smiled at his fiancé and took her hand in his. "We won't have any secrets from one another in our marriage."

Ryan was the first to speak. "Congratulations, you two. Henry, if anyone deserves a second chance at happiness, it's you. Carole, you're getting a fine man."

"Yes, I am." She looked at Henry, and her whole face lit up. "I'm going to do everything in my power to make him happy, and I hope to see more of the two of you, and Meredith, in the future."

"We'll see how that goes." Reagan cleared her throat, sat down, and continued. "Henry, if you're sure you don't mind, then I'm going to tell you both what happened last weekend."

"Of course."

"You know I'd been making trips to Maine to sell my watercolors for a few years. Well, we decided to relocate to a small town, Wentworth Cove, where we knew and trusted the gallery owner and his wife. They found us the perfect house to lease, and I enrolled Mere in school. She misses her friends here—and you, Henry—but she's already made some good friends there. I found out my landlady was a painter too, but had never sold any of her paintings. We talked her into letting us put on a one-woman show for her at the gallery. It was Sunday. During the event, I looked across the room…and locked eyes with Jared."

"It couldn't—" Henry protested. "In Maine?"

"Let me finish." She took a deep breath. "This isn't easy to tell you."

"Go ahead."

"I left immediately and went to what I considered a safe location and had a friend bring Mere to me."

"I can't believe he would just show up like that," Henry interjected. "He knows he isn't supposed to leave the state."

"I couldn't believe it either, but there was no mistaking those eyes. He had tried to disguise himself. Have you seen him lately, Henry?"

"Not for a couple of weeks. The last time he was over, I noticed he hadn't shaved for a few days."

"He had a short beard when I saw him, and he'd cut his hair. He wore a ball cap and glasses."

"That doesn't sound like Jared at all. I've never seen him in glasses…or a ball cap. Are you sure?"

"I didn't want it to be him—probably even more than you don't want it to be him—but that's not the clincher. In fact, that's not the most convincing part of the evidence. Toward the end of the event, after Meredith and I had left, the artist who was being honored had a heart attack and the man I'd locked eyes with rushed over and started doing CPR. He shouted to someone to call 911 and to tell them to bring morphine and GTN. Who, besides a doctor, would have known to do all that? In all fairness, the paramedics and emergency room doctor said he saved her life with his quick response."

"That does put a different slant on it, I'll have to admit."

"It does for me too, Henry, but the fact remains that he left the state, and if his parole officer found out…"

"So that leads me to the question of the day…" Henry said.

Reagan shrugged. "Which is?"

"What are you going to do about it? The ball is in your court. But first, you have to make sure it was him. You can't be a hundred percent sure, can you? How would he have found out where you were?"

"That's what I thought at first," Ryan said, "but it's hard to refute the evidence."

"I'm trying to make it not true, I guess. He's doing so well. He's started a dog-walking business and it's growing by leaps and bounds. He's even had to hire a helper. And he's paid back some up-front money I gave him to get started."

"You asked how he found out where we'd moved," Reagan continued. "I wondered, too, but then I remembered I'm on the internet under Reagan Loper, and I sell Miss Carter's paintings on my website. A quick check of her name would have taken him to the local paper's website with all the information. It was a long shot in a way, but apparently he felt the possibility of seeing Mere was worth it."

"Did she see him?" Carole asked. "I'm sorry. I know I'm not a member of the family, but I'm a therapist, and I can imagine how this is affecting her."

"No, but she wanted to. She's well aware of what he did and that his illegal actions caused a death, but now she thinks he's redeemed himself by saving Miss Carter's life."

"A life for a life," Henry said, almost under his breath.

"You can look at it that way, Henry, but I can't. I have Meredith to think of," Reagan reminded him.

"Carole specializes in adolescents in her practice. Maybe she could shed some light on how a visit with him could affect Mere, either positively or negatively."

"Whether or not you decide to have me assess her, Reagan," Carole said, getting up to refill Henry's mug of cider, "I'd love to meet her. Henry has raved on and on about you two."

"What I really need to do now is talk to Jared. Not a visit I'm looking forward to, I can assure you."

"I understand," Henry said. "Well, you have his number. Were you afraid I wouldn't give it to you if you hit me with this news first?"

"This was not a conversation I wanted to have over the phone...not a conversation I wanted to have at all," Reagan said.

"Will you get back in touch after you've seen him?"

"Of course. And regardless of how it goes, I'll bring Mere soon...to see you, Henry and to meet you, Carole. And congratulations on your engagement. I'm truly happy for both of you."

Chapter Twenty-One

With trembling hands Reagan dialed the number of the man she hadn't spoken to in over seven years. The man with whom she'd once shared a bed, a daughter, and a life. She'd asked Maggie for only Friday and Saturday off and had to return to Maine on Sunday, so she thought it best to try to make arrangements to see Jared on Saturday. That is, if he would agree to meet with her. He'd probably assume she had Meredith with her, and she wouldn't tell him anything different.

She hoped he'd answer because she didn't want to leave a message and wonder when and if he would call back. He answered on the first ring.

"Jared's Dog-walking Service. Jared speaking."

"Hi, Jared. It's Reagan."

The silence seemed like an eternity. Finally, he said, "Reagan. What do you want? After all these years."

"I'm in town for a couple of days and was wondering if we could talk."

"Well, that's what we're doing, isn't it? You've already said more words to me than you said in the last seven years."

"Could we meet? I'd like to speak to you in person." Another long silence, and Reagan wondered if Jared was trying to figure out how to weasel out because he knew she'd recognized him on Sunday. "Jared?"

"Seven years and now I'm supposed to drop everything and see you on your timetable."

"Tomorrow? I won't be in town long."

"I work on Saturday. Yes. I have a job, and I'm a self-supporting citizen of New York City again."

"Your lunch break, maybe? It'll take just a few minutes." The phone was on speaker, and Ryan nodded his approval.

"Why do you want to see me now? Dad said you moved. So you wouldn't run into me, I figured. But now you're trying to arrange a meeting? Why?"

"I'd rather tell you in person. What's a good location for you tomorrow?"

"Caffe Reggio on MacDougal. Eleven-thirty."

"I'll see you there."

"With Meredith?"

"Not this time," Reagan said and immediately disconnected the call. "Oh, Ry. I can't believe I'm doing this. Why did he have to show up just when things were going so well?"

"Were you really surprised? I mean you moved all the way up to Maine to get away from him. You must have thought he'd try to find you or you would have stayed where you were. Where Mere had friends."

"I'm just surprised he was able to locate us so quickly. I let my guard down by putting Ida's paintings on my website. I never imagined he could track us through her."

"Will you be able to sleep tonight?"

"I don't know. Hope so."

"I'm in the room right next door. Knock on the wall if you need anything."

"What would I do without you?" Reagan asked.

"You'd be fine. You're stronger than you think. You're just feeling vulnerable right now."

"Good night."

"Night. See you at eight-thirty for breakfast? There's a buffet downstairs."

"Sure. If I can eat…"

Reagan woke to a cold and dreary day that mirrored her mood. Opening the curtains in her hotel room produced little to no light, so she switched on a couple of lamps and jumped in the shower. A hot shower was just what she needed, and Reagan wished she could stay forever so she wouldn't have to confront her ex-husband. But she knew she had to get it over with or her life—and Meredith's—would never be normal again. She would always wonder when he'd show up. And whether he'd try to talk to his daughter the next time.

By the time she got out of the shower and was towel-drying her hair, she still hadn't decided what to do about the fact he'd left the state and blatantly violated his parole orders. Would she contact his parole officer and hope he'd be sent back to prison, or hold that action over his head as a way to keep him away from Wentworth Cove? And would the threat really keep him away? He hadn't seemed to mind taking a risk when he drove the five hours to Maine a few days ago. And Reagan couldn't be sure just how much of a risk taker he was after seven years in prison.

She finished drying her hair, put on a little makeup, slipped on jeans and a sweater, gathered her purse and coat, and headed down to the hotel restaurant to meet Ryan.

"How long have you been here?" she asked when she spotted him in the lobby.

"Not long. Still on my first cup of coffee. Ready to get some breakfast?"

"I guess I should eat a little."

"Mere texted me last night," Ryan said after they'd gone through the buffet line and seated themselves at a table in the corner.

"Yeah. Me too. Wanted to know if I'd seen him yet. What did she text you about?"

"Wanted to know if I'd take her to the father-daughter Christmas dance her school is sponsoring."

"Oh, Ry. That makes me so sad. But I'm glad she has you. When is it?"

"That's the problem. You know I'd do it if I could, but it's the same weekend I have to be in Denver for a meeting with a prospective client who's moving his headquarters to Boston and wants to talk with me about designing the building. I can't pass up an opportunity like that. I'm sad that I can't be there for her, though."

"That's okay. Don't worry about it. You have your life and your career to think about. You've been there for us throughout this whole ordeal. And look. You're here for me now. Mere will live over it. Sometimes life just throws us a few curve balls, but we still have to stay in the batter's box and keep swinging."

"Look at you with the baseball analogy." Ryan leaned back in his chair and smiled.

Reagan laughed. "Yeah, I don't know where that came from."

"It's good to hear you laugh. You feeling okay about today?"

"Better now. I just have to remember that I have the upper hand. If I forget that when we're talking to him, kick me under the table or something."

"I'll do something to remind you. Hey. Since we're here and have a couple of hours before we have to meet him, what do you want to do?"

"I'd love to go by the gallery, but I don't want to run into anyone who would start asking questions. It looks like the weather is clearing up a little. I could use a walk. That's one thing I miss about the city. Maybe in the spring I can find some hiking trails."

"You're fortunate to be able to take off yesterday and today," Ryan said. "Your boss seems nice."

"She's very nice. I think I'll get her something from the city now that I think about it. I told her everything. Figured if I was going to ask for a couple of days, she deserved to know why. It's going to get out anyway. No way I can stop it now. So…you were impressed with Maggie?"

"I just said she seems nice…but now that you mention it… Too bad she lives an hour and a half from Boston."

"Brett lives an hour and a half from Wentworth Cove, but he makes the drive often to check on his aunt."

"To check on his aunt, huh?" Ryan teased.

Reagan rolled her eyes, but she could feel her cheeks getting warm and wondered if Ryan noticed.

Brett Mason was just starting his weekend with plans for lunch with friends and a matinee afterwards when his phone vibrated in his pocket. Meredith Hart. Why would she be calling?

"Meredith. Good morning."

"Hi."

"How's everything in the Cove?"

"Okay, I guess."

"Are you all right?"

"I'm fine. I just wanted to ask you a question."

"Sure. Shoot."

"Well… My uncle can't take me to the father-daughter Christmas dance that my school is having because he'll be in Denver that weekend."

"I'm sorry to hear that," Brett said, wondering where this was going.

"And, well… I was wondering… I mean if you're going to be here checking on Miss Carter anyway… Well, I was wondering if you would take me."

"Oh, Meredith. There's nothing I'd like more than to go to that dance with you…but I don't think your mom would be too happy about that. I'm kind of on her naughty list right now."

"I know that so I asked her. She said it's okay," Meredith assured him. "If you want to, that is. But not to pressure you. So this is me not pressuring you."

"Well…in that case, I would love to be your escort to the Christmas dance. What weekend is it? I'll make sure I'm there. Just text me all the details."

"You will? Thanks, Brett! It would be kind of embarrassing to be the only girl in the seventh grade who's not going. Now I don't have to worry about that."

"Is this a formal affair? Should I rent a tux?"

"No. They said to tell the dads to wear business casual…whatever that is."

"No problem. I can handle that just fine. When you know more, let me know what color your dress is…so we can color coordinate. It'll help me decide which sport coat to wear."

"Yeah, sure! I'll text you all the details. Thank you so much!"

"Thank *you*. I'm honored that you asked me, Mere."

So… Reagan must not be too mad at him after all, if she'd let him escort Meredith to a school dance. That thought filled him with new hope. And it might even put a new twist on a decision he had to make in the next few weeks.

Reagan and Ryan arrived at Caffe Reggio at eleven-twenty and asked for a table for three in the corner. They'd been there five minutes when he walked in. No cap, no glasses, no beard. But his hair was short. That was the one thing he couldn't change, and it confirmed what Reagan already knew. Jared had left the state of New York and violated his parole orders. She had him over a barrel. Being able to prove it might be another matter, however.

"Jared," Ryan said, standing and offering to shake his hand, but Jared's hands stayed in his jacket pockets.

"So. You wouldn't bring my daughter, but you brought him," he said to Reagan. "I feel like this is an ambush."

"Why would we try to ambush you, Jared? Would there be a reason?" Reagan asked.

"I don't know what you have on your mind these days…since we haven't spoken in over seven years…until yesterday. What's this about anyway?"

"Sit down, Jared, so we can talk," Ryan said.

"I don't know what this has to do with you anyway, Ryan. Everything that needs to be said about seeing my daughter is between Reagan and me. Why are you here?"

"Ryan's here because I asked him to come," Reagan said. "Would you sit down, please, so we can talk and keep this civil?"

A server finally ambled over and laid three menus on the table. "Can I get you guys anything to drink?"

After they'd ordered drinks and sandwiches and he'd walked away, Reagan started. "You know I recognized you Sunday, don't you?"

"Make mine to go," Jared shouted at the waiter over his shoulder. "What are you talking about, Reagan? You were in town last weekend too? I thought you moved away from the city. That's what Dad told me."

"You know what I'm talking about," Reagan insisted. "And, by the way, the ER doctor said you saved her life."

"It really would help if I knew what all that meant. But I don't. Ryan, since you're here, you want to jump in and explain what your sister is referring to? All I can get out of her are riddles."

"Okay, Jared," Ryan started. "A photographer at the event—"

"What event?"

"A photographer at the event," Reagan continued, "got a good shot of your face, and the editor of the local paper used a facial recognition app to match it to a photo of you." Reagan figured a little white lie wouldn't hurt her case and might help it. She held up the newspaper photo for him to see.

"Now you've gone off the deep end. As you can see, I have no beard, and you both know that I've never worn glasses or owned a ball cap."

"All of those things would make a good disguise, though, wouldn't they?" Ryan suggested.

"I guess so—if someone wanted to disguise himself— which I do not. Where was this event supposed to have taken place?"

Reagan jumped back in. "Out-of-state."

"Well, there it is. You know I can't leave the state."

"Here's the deal, Jared." Reagan took a deep breath and continued, feeling a renewed resolve. "I'm not going to be unreasonable, but I can prove you violated your parole. If we're going to do this, we're going to do it on my terms. If you ever want to see Meredith again, actually if you want to remain a free man, you're going to cooperate with me."

"What exactly are your terms?"

Reagan gave him a glare that caused her blue eyes to blaze. "If you'll stay in New York…and never show up again where I live…I won't tell your parole officer where you went and what you did. However, if you don't abide by those guidelines…well, I think you know how serious I am and what I'll do."

"What about Meredith? You might have legal custody, thanks to a black-robed feminist, but she's my daughter too."

"I'll think about letting you see her at Henry's house with both Henry and me there...once or twice a year. But if I ever see you out-of-state again—"

"I think you've made your point."

"I'll be in touch. And, by the way, Miss Carter wanted me to thank you for taking the risk to come to her aid when she had the heart attack. She knows your quick thinking and acting saved her life." Another little...well, she just thought of it as an improvisation this time.

"Whatever..." Jared grabbed his sandwich and stalked out.

"You were awesome, Rea," Ryan said when Jared was out the door of the café. "What's this about Miss Carter wanting to—"

"I made that part up," Reagan admitted. "It seemed to be the right thing to say because I'm sure that's how she feels. It's a good thing this isn't a glass top table or you would've seen both my legs shaking. Did I sound nervous?"

"Not at all. I'm so proud of you. He knows you have him. I think he'll behave. Are you really going to let him see Mere?"

"I have to, don't you think? Not for him, but for her. She wanted to see him last Sunday. Brett says if I keep them apart now, Mere's curiosity will turn into resentment. And if Henry and I are both there..."

"Brett says, huh?" Ryan raised his eyebrows at his sister, who just shook her head. "I'd invite Carole too. She impressed me."

"You're right. I'm so happy for Henry. She seems very nice."

"Well then. I'm glad that's over. We have some free time now. Let's go find something for your boss. I'm thinking maybe a silk scarf...to match her eyes."

Chapter Twenty-Two

Reagan had been furious when she got back to Lonewild and Meredith announced Brett was taking her to the school dance on Saturday night. She thought she'd made herself clear the last time she and Brett had talked. Apparently not.

She'd dialed his number as soon as Meredith had left of the room. "I can't believe you told Mere you'd take her to the dance when you know how we left things," she said when he answered the phone.

"But Meredith said—" He'd stopped short, realizing for the first time what had happened. Meredith lied to him when she told him Reagan had okayed his taking her to the dance.

"Meredith said *what*? She played on your sympathy again, didn't she?"

"She's looking forward to it, Reagan, and she'll be embarrassed if she's the only girl at school who isn't there because she doesn't have a dad. Just let me take her," Brett pleaded, "and then I'll keep my distance. And if she wants to talk about her dad, I'll shut down the conversation. I won't interfere. You have my promise."

Reagan had meant to say no, but somehow it had come out as a yes, and he'd be there any minute. She wondered how she'd feel when she saw him again.

She didn't have to wonder long. The front doorbell rang, and she answered it to find Brett looking better than ever in tan slacks and a dark green sport coat. She hoped he couldn't tell she was rattled by his presence.

"I expected you to come in through the kitchen like you always do." Lame, she thought, but she was suddenly incapable of saying anything clever or meaningful.

"That's not a proper way to pick up a young lady to go to a Christmas dance." And as soon as he'd said it, Meredith floated down the stairs looking like an angel in a knee-length dress of white satin and lace.

"Hi, Brett." She beamed.

"Wow! You're a picture of loveliness, young lady. It's a good thing there won't be seventh grade guys there. I might have to set a few knuckleheads straight," he said, laughing. "Here's something for you." He took a corsage of red rosebuds out of its white box and put it on her wrist.

"Thank you. It's *so* pretty. And you look cool too."

"It's very nice, Brett. You didn't have to do that," Reagan said.

"My pleasure. We're going to have a great time. The dance is over at ten. I'll have her home by ten-thirty at the latest, Mom."

"Bye, Mom," Meredith said with a quick hug, and they were gone.

What do I do now? Reagan had thought many times about having a teenager in a couple of years, a daughter who would want to start dating in a few years, and about the probability of Meredith married at some point, but she hadn't thought about it in relation to what she would do when she was alone...with no daughter, no husband, no anyone with whom she was emotionally connected. But after the ordeal with Jared, Reagan knew she would have a hard time ever completely trusting anyone again.

It was a fairly mild night for December in New England, so she decided to take a stroll down the path to the water. She and Meredith had been down to the ocean a couple of times, but she hadn't ventured there alone. And never at night. There were floodlights on the back of the house, and solar lanterns lighted the pathway, but she grabbed a jacket and a flashlight just in case.

The tide was high and waves crashed violently against the cliff. The breath of the ocean was coming in and going out with such regularity that Reagan wished she could breathe with the same unwavering assurance. Even in its violence, it remained steady, constant, rhythmic. Since she'd seen Jared at the gallery, her breathing had been mercurial, changeable depending on her thoughts at the moment. Sometimes she'd remember that she was in control and could have him sent back to prison, and the breaths would come methodically and easily. Then she would think about how the situation had changed her idyllic new life at Lonewild—and her friendship with Brett—and the intake and output of air was unpredictable, sometimes coming in short, shallow gasps.

In the distance Reagan could see the light from the Goat Island lighthouse that was perched on a small, rocky island in Wentworth Cove Harbor and had been shining and beckoning people to safety since 1833. Though it had been automated since 1990, she could imagine the lighthouse keeper, whose job it was to lead ships to safety, being able to sleep soundly at night, knowing he'd done his job by protecting the sea captains. Would she be able to continue to protect her daughter so easily from the dangers of the world? Not only Jared, but all the other unsure and unsafe situations she would face in the future?

And how would Meredith feel when she found out she wouldn't be able to continue her friendship with Brett? He'd apparently come to mean more to her than Reagan had realized. She could have asked David to take her to the dance. After all, she'd known him a lot longer. But she didn't. She asked Brett.

And Reagan had no intention for forgiving him for saying yes without consulting her first.

When Reagan got back to the house, she decided to pass the time by cooking. Besides painting, it was the activity she could count on to calm her nerves. Her second creative outlet. She was taking a sour cream pound cake out of the oven when the doorbell rang and she looked at the clock on the wall. Ten-twenty already? Impossible. How had three hours passed so quickly? In spite of her doubts about allowing Meredith to go to the dance with Brett, Reagan realized she'd actually enjoyed her time alone.

Meredith was animated when she came in and couldn't wait to tell her mother all about the dance. "Brett was the coolest dad there! He knew every dance. And he taught everybody how to line dance."

"That's nice, Mere," Reagan replied reservedly.

"Well, I'll be off," Brett said, knowing he'd already overstayed his welcome by just being there.

"You don't have to go now," Meredith said. "What do I smell? Did you bake, Mom?"

"Just a pound cake."

"Brett, don't you want to stay and have some?" Meredith asked.

Brett cut his eyes at Reagan, whose expression seemed to say, *Don't even think about it.* "I really need to run, but I had a great time tonight, Mere. It was an honor to escort the prettiest young lady at Kennebunk Middle School." And he was out the door.

"You weren't very friendly, Mom," Meredith said as soon as Brett was gone.

"It's complicated."

"Are you still mad at him for taking my side when I wanted to be able to see Dad?"

"Sweetheart, we haven't known Brett very long, and he hasn't known us very long. He doesn't understand the whole situation, so I don't think he has a right to voice an opinion. I also think he should have talked with me before he agreed to take you to the dance. Especially after the way we ended things the last time we talked."

"Well, maybe…" She hesitated.

"Maybe what?"

"Never mind," Meredith said. "I think I'll go to bed now. I'm tired."

"Okay. I *am* glad you got to go to the dance. And I *am* glad you had a good time. Good night. Love you."

"I love you too, Mom."

The next morning Meredith got a text from Brett.

We need to talk.

I know.

Call me when you can.

OK.

She immediately dialed Brett's number and he answered on the first ring. "You know why we're talking, don't you?" he asked.

"Yeah."

"You weren't exactly truthful to me when you told me your mom said you could ask me to the dance, were you? And now you're not being exactly truthful to your mom, are you?"

"No."

"So what are you going to do about it? What's the right thing to do? Do you think it's my place to tell her...or yours?"

"You're not going to tell her, are you?"

"No. I'm not."

"Thanks!" Meredith let out a sigh of relief.

"But you are."

"I am?"

"Mere, do you remember when you asked me if I like, 'like' your mom? When I was taking you to the library?"

"Yes."

"Well, I do like, 'like' her. Do you think it's fair to me that she stays mad because she thinks I went behind her back and did something she might not allow if she knew? Remember when you wanted me to take her on a date? Well, I'd like to do that. But do you think she'd go?"

"No."

"Do you think she might go if she knew I was acting in good faith and thought she'd said it was okay for me to take you to the dance?"

"Yeah."

"So what do you think you should do?" Brett felt a strong desire to protect her, but he also knew she needed to learn from this situation and he had no intention of letting Reagan continue to think he'd gone behind her back.

"It'll be so hard. I've never lied to her before. She'll be sad. And she'll probably ground me. I've never been grounded."

"Meredith, sometimes we have to do the hard things and take the consequences. You'll get over the grounding. But, believe it or not, you'll feel better after you get it all out in the open. Your mom loves you, and I think she'll be glad that you told her the truth…even if it was a little late in coming."

"I know. And it's not fair to you that she thinks you're a bad guy. 'Cause you're not. You took me to the dance, and it was a lot of fun… Brett?"

"Yeah?"

"I wish my dad had been more like you. I wish he hadn't done all those things that hurt people."

"Thank you, Mere," he said, swallowing the lump in his throat and gathering his thoughts. "That's just about the greatest compliment I've ever received."

"You want me to text you after I tell her?"

"That would be great."

"Okay. Bye."

Chapter Twenty-Three

Reagan had slept a fitful sleep, her mind trying to reconcile the Brett she thought she knew with the Brett who promised Meredith something without consulting her. Though she'd tried to mask her emotions, she knew he must have been able to tell how unhappy she was with him last night. She hadn't been able to eat anything since she woke up, but she was on her second cup of coffee when her phone rang and Elizabeth's name popped up.

"Hi, Elizabeth."

"Good morning. I just wanted to tell you that I'm so glad you decided to let Meredith ask Brett to take her to the dance. I know she would have felt left out if she couldn't have gone. Of course, David would have taken her since her uncle couldn't, but she really wanted it to be Brett."

"What do you mean I *let* her ask Brett?" Reagan asked. "I had no idea she was going to ask him."

"You didn't?"

"Why do you sound surprised?"

"Brett wasn't going to say yes because he knew how you felt about his interference in the Jared thing, but Meredith… Um… I think I've spoken out of turn. Forget what I just said. David told me weeks ago not to get involved. But I *am* glad she got to go…no matter how it happened."

"Thanks. Could I call you back later? I think I need to talk to someone."

"Sure."

Reagan absentmindedly tucked her hair behind her left ear as the realization hit her. A light-bulb moment. "Brett totally took the blame, didn't he? He found out she hadn't talked to me, but he didn't say anything to get her in trouble."

"That's what it's sounding like."

"Thanks for letting me know."

"He's a good guy, Reagan," Elizabeth said. "Go easy on him."

"Mom?" Meredith said as she came downstairs for the first time Saturday morning.

"Yeah?"

"I need to talk to you."

"Okay." Reagan wasn't planning to make this easy for her daughter.

"Well… You know how you're mad at Brett because he said yes when I asked him to take me to the dance?"

"Yes. He shouldn't have done that."

"Well… You really shouldn't be mad at him."

"Oh? Really? Why is that?"

"He thought it was okay with you."

"Why would he think that when he knew I was upset with him?"

"I might have—"

"You *might* have *what?*"

"I wasn't truthful with him. I told him you said it was okay." Tears burned Meredith's eyes as she confessed. "I'm sorry, Mom. I know you're going to ground me or something."

"And you let me continue to believe he just took it on himself to say he'd take you without talking to me first?"

"That was wrong too. I'm sorry. None of this was his fault."

"Does he know you're telling me this?"

"He's the one who talked me into it. He said sometimes we have to do hard things regardless of the consequences. Am I grounded?"

"I'll have to think about it. But I know one thing. Brett isn't. I've been very unfair to him, and I have to fix it."

"Maybe he likes pound cake," Meredith suggested, as she sniffed and wiped tears from her cheeks. "He told me to text him as soon as I talked to you. Want me to ask him?"

"No. I started this unfair judgment of him. I'll deal with it. Sometimes we have to do hard things, right? Meanwhile, I think you need to go to your room to think about what you did. As far as I know, you've never been dishonest before. And this had better be the last time. Text him quickly and then leave your phone with me for a while. I'll come up and talk to you later."

As soon as he'd read Meredith's text, Brett's phone rang. "Mr. Mason?"

"Yes."

"This is Rhonda Briggs from Sunshine Assisted Living Center."

"Is my aunt okay?"

"She didn't come to breakfast this morning, so we went to check on her. She was lying on her bed with a smile on her face, but we couldn't wake her so we called 911. Mr.

Mason, I'm sorry to have to tell you this, but the paramedics said she went peacefully in her sleep. I hope you can take solace in knowing that. The coroner has been here. Another heart attack, he suspects."

A seasoned reporter, Brett was accustomed to receiving bad news, but this took him off guard. "Where is she now?" he asked after he had partially recovered.

"We're waiting on instructions from you to tell us where you want us to have her taken."

"Could I gather my thoughts and call you back in a couple of minutes?"

"Of course. I know this was unexpected, in a way. She seemed to be doing so well since that scare at the gallery."

"I'll be in touch soon," he assured her.

Unexpected was an understatement. Brett supposed he'd expected Ida to live forever. At least not be gone this suddenly when she seemed to have bounced back from the first heart attack so effortlessly. He wasn't prepared to lose the last connection to his parents and grandparents.

What do I need to do first? Contact a funeral home? I know she wanted to be cremated, but I don't know of a crematory in the area. Maybe the facility will know of one. Who else needs to be notified? Isaac? He'll put an obit in the paper, and that will take care of most of the people she knows.

But Brett had told Rhonda Briggs he'd call her back soon, so he dialed the number she'd used to call him. "Ms. Briggs, this is Brett Mason. I was wondering if you know of a crematory in the area."

"I know a couple. Would you like me to call one for you? Her wish was to be cremated?"

"Yes. It's stated in her will too. I'm the executor, and there's a copy at her estate attorney's office there in Kennebunk...Kyle Newsome."

"Would you like to see her before she is removed from the facility?"

"Actually, I'd like to remember her the way she was the last time I saw her…full of life and handing out advice to anyone who would listen."

"That she did. That she did," Rhonda agreed. "We're all going to miss her around here. Such a presence. Such a positive attitude. We could use more like her here."

"Thank you for calling the crematory. Tell them to invoice me. You have my information?"

"We have your address and phone number. Yes. They'll get in touch with you when they have the cremated remains ready to be picked up."

"I know she offered to pay to have the sign outside changed from Sundown to Sunshine. I'll certainly still honor that. Just let me know how much it is, and it will come out of her estate."

"I will, and thank you for remembering. Take care, Mr. Mason, and let us know when you've made arrangements for a memorial service. There are some people here who will want to go. We'll take a couple of vans."

As Brett was putting his phone down, he looked again at Meredith's text.

I told her everything. She doesn't blame you for anything now. I have to go to my room without my phone for a while.

What a day! I feel like I'm on an emotional roller coaster. Should I call Reagan or hope she calls me? I could tell her about Aunt Ida. I really should. But what's the hurry? I'd like to know if she's going to make the first move. That will be telling since I'm not sure where I stand with her anyway. Would she be interested if we hadn't had the misunderstanding?

As if on cue, Brett's phone rang and he picked it back up. *Well, Reagan. I was just thinking about you. No. Play it cool, Mason.*

"Hello, Reagan."

"Hi," she said sheepishly. "I was wondering if you like pound cake?"

Play it cool, but not too cool. "Have you ever known me to turn down food of any kind?"

"You're still at David's, right?"

"I'm actually staying in the apartment in the back of the gallery, but yeah. I'm still in town. And Reagan...I have some news to tell you. Do you want me to tell you now or..."

"Can you..." The words caught in her throat. "Can you come over?"

"For pound cake? Any time of the day or night."

"Brett, I owe you a huge apology," Reagan said as she opened the kitchen door. "Meredith told me what she did...but you already know that, don't you?"

"She texted me, yeah. I'm glad she talked to you about it. Where is she now?"

"Still in her room...thinking about what she did, I hope. She owes you an apology too, for putting you in a bad situation."

"She already apologized to me. And thank you for the apology. I didn't like thinking our friendship was over. And I don't remember which way it is, but one of us still owes the other a surf and turf... But listen. I need to tell you something I found out this morning."

"What is it? You sound so serious," Reagan said, setting a large slice of pound cake on the table.

"Aunt Ida passed away in her sleep last night. They think it was another heart attack."

"What? Oh, Brett. I'm so sorry. How are you?"

"I've had a little time to get used to it now." He pulled out a chair and sat down at the table. "But I was shocked at first. I mean, I talked to her a couple of days ago, and she sounded so good. Said everything was fine."

Reagan sat down across from him. "We don't have the guarantee of a tomorrow, do we? None of us do. And occasionally we get reminded of that. This is one of those times. I didn't know her long, but I will miss her. She was quite an inspiration. I don't guess you've had time to make any arrangements yet. I'll be glad to help with anything you need...especially since I'm here and you're probably going to have to go back to Augusta tomorrow...or soon anyway."

"Thanks. I might take you up on that."

"It seems like all I'm doing today is telling you I'm sorry," Reagan said. "I hope Meredith's learned her lesson. I know I have. I'm not going to be so quick to judge or distrust people. Especially people I care about."

"You know, Reagan," Brett said, setting aside his fork and putting his arms on the table, "I was Meredith's age when my parents were killed in a car wreck that left a teenage boy partially paralyzed. Word got around school that the accident was caused by my dad's excessive drinking at a company party. David was the first person who took up for me, and since he was big man on campus, so to speak—popular anyway—the talk gradually subsided. I know what it's like to try to start over in a new school at twelve years of age with something embarrassing like that hanging over your head. Kids can be cruel. And I wanted to give Meredith something positive that they could talk about rather than wondering why she couldn't come to the dance and possibly finding out about her dad's prison record. I think we accomplished that. She had a great time and seems to be well liked. I know that doesn't excuse what she did, but maybe it puts some perspective on it."

"It does. But we've always been able to tell each other everything, and it's hard to realize that she's almost a teenager and won't always want to confide in me. I wish she'd asked me if it was okay to invite you."

"Would you have said yes?"

"I don't know," Reagan confessed. "Maybe not. I was so upset and confused about Jared's unexpected appearance. I don't know how I would have reacted."

"I guess she didn't want to take that chance."

Reagan smiled. "She's lucky to have you on her side."

"I'm on your side too," he assured her. "If there are sides in this. You've both become pretty special to me."

"I'm not forgetting that you just found out about Ida. Is there anything I can help with today? What about writing an obituary and getting it in the paper?"

"I need to talk to Isaac about that...and about another matter. Today, in fact. Guess I'd better go. Thanks for the cake. And the talk. I was feeling pretty rotten."

"Better now?" Reagan asked.

"Yeah. You?"

"Definitely."

"I'll let you tell Meredith about Aunt Ida. I know they were fond of each other."

"I hadn't thought about that, but yeah, she'll be sad about her passing."

"Call you later?" Brett asked as he stood up and put on his jacket.

"I'd like that."

Chapter Twenty-Four

Brett was shaken by the news of his aunt, but his visit with Reagan had lifted his spirits. In a moment of clarity, he realized just how much her attitude since Jared's appearance at the gallery had affected him. Which, he supposed, translated to the fact that he cared more about her than he realized. But as much as he would like to, he couldn't sit around thinking about Reagan Hart all day. So he dialed the number of the man he felt should be notified first.

"Isaac? Brett Mason."

"I knew I'd hear from you today. So sorry to learn of Ida's passing. Rather unexpected, wasn't it?"

"A little, but when it's my time to go...well, I can't think of a better way to leave this earth than in my sleep with a smile on my face."

"Indeed. Indeed."

"I figured you'd know already. You've always had your finger on the pulse of this community. How do you do that?" Brett asked. "And how will anyone be able to fill your shoes?"

"I'm just a crusty old curmudgeon. But this line of questioning leads me to believe you've been mulling over my proposition, eh?"

"It would be hard not to think about an offer like that. I'm leaning in a certain direction but not able to give you a final answer just yet. It would be a huge change for me, you know."

"Of course it would. And that's why you should seriously consider it. A political reporter, even an excellent one like you, can get jaded from all that dishonesty and corruption. I mean, have you ever known a politician to be completely clean?"

"Very few. And, unfortunately, they don't usually get elected."

"Just wrong on so many levels. My Miriam is one of the few, though."

"She certainly is. Wentworth Cove will miss her too. I was actually calling to see if you need any information for the obit. Or if you want me to write it."

"I've started it, but I'd certainly like it to have your fingerprint on it. Why don't I send you what I have, and you take it from there. Discard anything you don't want and add what you want. I'd like to run it in Monday's paper. Not that there will be anyone left who doesn't know of her passing, but some people would just like to read about her fascinating life. Could you have it to me by around three tomorrow?"

"Sure. And Isaac...I want you to know I'm seriously considering your generous offer, but there are some details I need to iron out before I can say anything for sure."

"Take your time, my boy. We still have a few weeks until the end of the year."

As soon as Brett ended his call with Isaac Weiler, he phoned Reagan.

"Is Meredith out of her room yet?"

"Yeah. I told her about Ida. She's very sad."

"Is she grounded?"

"No. Thanks to you, we had a good discussion, and I think she's learned her lesson. She was quite contrite and cried when we talked about it."

"Good. What are you two ladies doing this afternoon?" Brett asked.

"No plans. Why?"

"I would like to take you to someplace special and then to dinner...if you're up for an adventure."

"Well..."

"It's a date. Wear your warmest clothes. We'll be outside for a little while."

"Where are we going?"

"To rediscover our childhoods..."

"I imagine my childhood was quite different from yours. Which one are we going to rediscover?"

"Well, mine for sure and maybe the beginning of a tradition for you and Mere."

"That would be nice. We could use some fun today. Any hints?"

"Nope. Can you be ready by four?"

"Can do."

"See you then."

"Where are we going, Brett?" Meredith asked with an expectancy in her voice as she handed him a handmade card.

"You'll know pretty soon. What's this?" he asked, ushering them into the car.

"Just something I drew for you."

Brett opened the card to see a rainbow reflected in a teardrop: *Sometimes you can see a rainbow through tears. Thank you for making me do the hard things and for not holding it against me that I wasn't honest with you. You're the coolest! Meredith*

"Thank you, Mere. I'll treasure this forever," Brett said, smiling at her in the rearview mirror. "Buckle up, ladies. We're going hunting."

"Um… We're doing what?" Reagan asked. "I hope you don't mean we're going to kill Bambi."

"Oh, no. No guns this time. Just my trusty saw in the back of the vehicle."

"Saw? Wait a minute. Are we—"

"Yep. We're on a hunt for the biggest, most beautiful Christmas tree Lonewild has ever seen."

"We've never had a real tree," Meredith said.

"What? Never?"

"It's true," Reagan affirmed. "I was just about to bring down our little artificial tree from the upstairs guest room closet. Just hadn't gotten around to it yet."

"Well, that's good. I have a feeling an apartment-sized tree might be dwarfed by twelve-foot high ceilings."

"So where are we going to get this Lonewild-sized tree?" Reagan asked, laughing.

"Nottingham's Christmas Tree Farm. The same place my grandparents and Aunt Ida took me when I was a kid. They've been in business forever. We always got two. One for Lonewild, and one for my grandparents' smaller house. Aunt Ida loved Christmas better than anybody and couldn't wait to get her tree up so she could decorate it. Of course, I always enjoyed helping because the event involved cookies and hot chocolate and Christmas music."

"Then I think we should carry on that tradition," Meredith said. "In honor of Miss Carter. Especially the cookies and hot chocolate."

"Selfie time!" Meredith announced as they stood in the living room admiring their handiwork. "Mom, you stand right there in front of the tree. Brett stand by her, and I'll get on the other side of you."

She extended her selfie stick as far as it would go to take in as much of the tree as she could. "Wait! We need to turn the tree lights on… Okay… Say *Merry Christmas*!" Click!

"Text me that pic, Mere," Brett said. "Hey. Turn off the music for just a minute."

"Okay and okay. Done…and done. But why?"

"Listen."

"What are we listening for?" Reagan asked.

"Just listen… There it is again… Hear that?"

"I heard something," Meredith said. "What is it, Brett?"

"You two stay in here while I check on something outside."

"Well, be careful. Are you sure you want to go out there by yourself right now?"

"Sure. If it's what I think it is, I'll be fine. If not, well…it was nice knowing you lovely ladies."

Reagan reached in a drawer and took out a flashlight. "Take this."

He was gone about three minutes, and when he came back in, his jacket was wrapped around something besides just his chest. A small bulge, but a bulge nonetheless. Before he could unzip his jacket, a muffled sound came from the area of the protrusion.

A whimper?

"A puppy! It's a puppy, isn't it? Let me see!" Meredith was jumping around.

Brett pulled the white ball of fur out of his jacket and laid the puppy in her arms. "That it is."

"Mom! Look. I've always wanted a puppy. Remember when I used to ask you for one and you said we couldn't get one because we lived in an apartment? We're not in an apartment now."

"Don't get too attached, Mere. That puppy must belong to someone. He's—she's?—cute, though. No collar or tag?"

"Nope," Meredith said.

"We'll have to see if he's chipped. And put an ad in the paper to see if someone's missing him."

"You can do all that," Brett inserted, "but if I had to guess, I'd say someone dropped this cutie off on the side of the road and *she* wandered up to the house."

"Daisy!" Meredith exclaimed. "I've always wanted a dog named Daisy."

"Why Daisy?" Brett asked.

"Because that's my favorite flower. And look. She's white like a daisy. It's perfect." Meredith sat down and put the puppy on the floor. Daisy tottered over and rested her chin on Meredith's foot.

Reagan gave Brett a look that said, *It's too late now. She's ours.*

"Looks like Santa came early," Brett said, snapping a picture with his phone.

Reagan, knowing it was a done deal, said, "I have some cooked chicken in the refrigerator. I'll see if she's hungry. She'll need a bowl of water too. But first thing in the morning, I'm going to take her to the nearest vet, get her checked out, and see if she's chipped. If she isn't, chances are she doesn't have anyone looking for her. How old do you think she is?"

He looked thoughtful and ran his fingers through his short-cropped hair. "I'm not an expert, but my guess would be around six to nine months."

"She's so white she could get lost in the snow. I think we should get her a bright red collar. But what are we going to do with her while I'm at school and you're at work, Mom?"

"I'll be staying in the gallery apartment for a few more days to wrap up the arrangements for Aunt Ida's memorial service," Brett chimed in. "Why don't you bring her to me before you go to work, Reagan? After all, I feel slightly responsible for this situation."

"And you should." She smiled at him. "But if you hadn't heard her and gone out to look, I don't know what might have happened to her."

Chapter Twenty-Five

Daisy settled in at Lonewild as easily as Reagan and Meredith had. She wasn't chipped, and no one answered the ad Isaac put in the paper, so she took up residence in their home and in their hearts. Following Ida's memorial service and after Brett had gone back to Augusta, Maggie told Reagan to bring Daisy to the bookstore during her shift, and they set up a crate in the office and took turns walking her.

"Let me see if I have this right," Maggie said one day as Reagan was putting Daisy in her crate. "Brett took you and Meredith to cut down a Christmas tree at Nottingham's, helped you decorate it, heard Daisy whimper outside the house, and went out and brought her in."

"That about sums it up."

"Hmmm… Has he said anything about what he'll do with Lonewild now that he owns it? At least, I suppose he does. Miss Carter didn't have anyone else to leave it to."

"We haven't talked about it, but I don't know why he would want to live there since he works in Augusta. I guess he won't have a reason to come to the Cove now that Ida's gone. That's kind of sad."

"I'd say he has two very good reasons to come back often. Three, actually," Maggie said, pointing to Daisy, who lay curled up in her crate.

"I wish that was true, but I'm not sure…"

"Maybe you have to make it true. Does he know how you feel? If not, you need to let him know. He had his heart broken once. I'm sure he doesn't want it to happen again by assuming."

"I wonder if he'd want to go to the Christmas Eve candlelight service tomorrow night. Mere wants to go. As a matter of fact, I was going to ask you if you'd like to attend with us. Ryan will be here tomorrow. I'm sure he'd be glad to see you again."

"Really?" Maggie's face lit up.

"Oh, yeah. One hundred percent."

"Then I'd love to! Go call Brett before the shop gets busy!"

As soon as Brett had accepted Reagan's invitation to join her, Meredith, Maggie, and Ryan at the Christmas Eve service, he picked up the phone to call Isaac. He'd been back and forth on whether to accept his generous offer. A desire to slow down, to get away from politics and move back to a small town had been plusses. And so far the pros outweighed the cons. But Reagan's call sweetened the deal for him. If he planned to see where this relationship could go, he'd need to be closer than eighty-five miles, and he was getting tired of the hour and a half drive on I-95.

Isaac answered the office phone on the first ring. "You said by Christmas, Mason, but I get the feeling that two days before means good news."

"If you're sure, Isaac…"

"I gave it a lot of thought before I mentioned it to you. Also ran it by Miriam and she's in full agreement."

"Then I accept. I'd love to carry on your legacy at the *Courier*. And I promise to treat it with the same love and respect that you've done all these years it's been in your capable hands."

"I trust you'll do just that, my boy. Let me know when you can start. You'll be on your own the first of May. If you want to sign a contract, I'll have my attorney draw one up."

"No need. A handshake and a slice of pie will suffice. I'm turning in my resignation this afternoon. I'll be ready to shadow you starting the third week in January."

"I look forward to it."

The second call Brett made was to David asking him if he would consider leasing the gallery apartment to him for six months.

"Consider it done, but why? I was afraid we wouldn't see as much of you now that Ida's gone."

Brett told his friend of his impending career change and reason for moving back to Wentworth Cove. At least one of his reasons.

"That's good news, buddy. It'll be great to have you here. But why six months? Are you planning to move Reagan and Meredith out of Lonewild? Their lease isn't up in six months, is it?"

"That's not a consideration. Quite the opposite. Dave, I'm not spiking the football just yet, but it's time to see where this is going with Reagan. She's good at cooking and I'm good at eating. It's a match made in heaven." He and David both laughed. "In fact, she invited me to join her and her brother and Meredith at the Christmas Eve service tomorrow."

"Did she now? Well, they're all coming to our house for dinner on Christmas Day. Why don't you join us?"

"Love to…but only if I can bring something. I'll check with Elizabeth on that, though. I know who's planning the menu at your house."

"Let me put you on hold for a sec. It's Nathan." David was gone for only a couple of minutes. "I'm an uncle!" he announced proudly when he came back on. "Laura-Kate was born fifteen minutes ago! Mother and baby doing fine. I need to pick up Mom and get to the hospital. Can we continue this conversation later? Consider the apartment yours, though. And we'll count on you Christmas Day."

"Sure. Give them all my best."

Strains of "Joy to the World" filled the night air as people exited Wentworth Cove Community Church after the candlelight service. And, as if on cue, nickel-sized snowflakes began to gently fall to the frozen ground and blanket the lamp-lined streets of the Cove. If it continued all night, Reagan thought, it would be the most beautiful white Christmas she'd ever seen. One to top any she'd experienced in New York City. This village had captured her heart. Along with one of its former residents.

She held on to Brett's arm, and Maggie and Ryan followed close behind. Meredith, no doubt, had found Daniel and Landon and Molly.

"Is anyone hungry? I made a pot of beef stew, and Mere and I did a lot of baking today."

"I'm in," Brett said.

Ryan offered Maggie his arm. "Will you join us?"

"Mom," Meredith called from halfway across the parking lot, "Daniel and Molly and some of our other friends are going caroling, and Mrs. Parker said she'd bring me home around nine. May I go?"

"Sure. Have fun." Reagan couldn't get over how lucky they were to have met the Parkers, especially Daniel, who'd introduced Meredith to a lot of new friends. She hardly ever mentioned Maisie and Kelsey anymore.

The house glowed with the brightness and warmth of the holiday. The Lonewild-sized tree in the living room sparkled with colored lights and ornaments Reagan and Meredith had brought from New York and new ones they'd bought in Kennebunkport. Brett started a roaring fire while Reagan set the table and heated up the stew. Maggie and Ryan were talking on the sofa as if they were the only two people on earth. That made Reagan smile and inwardly congratulate herself.

Brett took the opportunity of being alone with Reagan in the kitchen for a few minutes to ask her a question he'd wanted to ask for several days. "I have Meredith's permission to take you on a proper date, and I'm not going to pass up a chance like this while I have you here alone. So, Ms. Hart…do you have plans for New Year's Eve?"

"That would be nice, Brett, but Ryan's staying through the first of the year…and I kind of hate to leave him alone on New Year's Eve."

"He won't be alone. Meredith said she would babysit him. And if I'm right in my journalistic sixth sense about what I've seen between him and Maggie tonight, there might be *two* ladies willing to make sure he doesn't feel alone."

"I know, right? I'm so glad they're enjoying each other's company. I had a feeling about them as soon as I met Maggie."

"Oh did you now? And did you have that same feeling about us?"

"It might have taken me a little longer, but I wasn't in a really good place emotionally when I met you because I'd found out so recently that Jared was getting out of prison early. I eventually came around though." She flashed him an encouraging smile.

"I don't think they're going to need us here, so how about an evening on the town in Portland? Eat on the harbor and take in the lights of the city? Watch the fireworks over the water?"

"I'd love to."

"It's a date then. I have a lot to tell you, but it can wait for a week."

"Maybe *it* can wait for a week, but I'm not sure *I* can. How about starting now?" Reagan begged. "That was a great hook, by the way, Mr. Reporter."

"Okay. One thing then. The other will have to wait."

"A compromise. Fair enough… So?"

"I talked with Aunt Ida's estate attorney yesterday, and he told me she'd recently added a codicil to her will that gives you all the rights to her paintings. Keep them, sell them, make prints. All the money from the watercolors goes to you. And rightly so," he added, "in my opinion."

"Wow! Seriously?"

"Seriously. But that's not all. Lonewild is mine now, but I can't sell it or do anything else with it as long as you want to live here. I hope you know I wouldn't have anyway. I think she knew that too, but she made doubly sure that you and Mere have a home here as long as you want." Reagan threw her arms around Brett. "I could get used to this," he said, just as Ryan and Maggie entered the kitchen.

"Sorry," Ryan said. "We smelled food and were getting kind of hungry…but if you're not ready for us…"

"It's ready." Reagan backed away from Brett and ran her hands down her skirt. "Let's eat."

Chapter Twenty-Six

New Year's Eve dinner was at Milo's Seafood House on the water in Portland Harbor, and Reagan and Brett finally had the lobster and steak they'd been joking about for months. Reagan dabbed at a bit of garlic butter on the side of her mouth. "I've made a decision about Jared."

"Yeah?"

"I don't want him to come here again, but I'm going to take Mere to see him a couple of times a year. We'll meet at his dad's house, and I'll always be there too. When she's eighteen, if she wants to see him by herself, that'll be her decision, but for now and the next five years, the visits will be chaperoned."

"That's a good compromise. And one of which I highly approve. Does she know?"

"I told her a couple of days ago. She was fine with it. I think she's mostly just curious. As soon as she sees him a couple of times, I'll be surprised if she's that eager to go back. Of course, she wants to see her grandfather more than anything else. They were very close and I feel bad that I cut that off completely."

"Everything's coming together for you then."

"It is. And you played a large role in bringing me to my senses about letting her see her dad. I know that and so does she."

"Glad I could be of service, ma'am," he said. "And I have some news for you too."

"Oh?"

"I've leased David's gallery apartment for six months."

"Really? Why? I thought you wouldn't be coming to Wentworth Cove as much now that Ida's gone."

"Two reasons, actually. One, the thought of a daily hour and a half commute twice a day doesn't appeal to me. And two, I think it's better for the editor of a local newspaper to live in the community."

"The editor of... You're telling me...what exactly? You're going to be the editor of the *Wentworth Cove Courier?*"

"That's what I'm telling you. Editor...as of the first of May...and eventually the owner."

"Really? That's *great* news!"

"I was hoping you'd feel that way. Besides...you might need someone to help you with that vegetable garden in the spring...and to teach you how to drive in snow."

"And Mere and I certainly can't finish off a sour cream pound cake by ourselves."

"More than happy to help with that."

"Interested in a walk along the water?" Brett asked after dinner and dessert. "We have a few minutes till the new year arrives and the fireworks start."

"Sure."

Brett took her hand in his as they strolled along the boardwalk. "I didn't tell you the main reason I told Isaac

I'd take over the paper," he said after they'd walked in silence for a while.

"No. You didn't."

"Moving back to the Cove sounded so appealing to me when Isaac first mentioned it because I love being with you…and when I'm away from you, I'm thinking about, and plotting, the next time we'll be together. When I'm in Augusta, I feel like I'm a thousand miles away."

"That's the way it feels to me too. Like you're too far away. I love the way I feel safe with you…knowing you'll never put me or Meredith at risk…and you're always thinking of ways for us to have fun together. I love that you care about my girl."

"Actually, I care very much about your daughter." Brett stopped and turned toward Reagan. "And I'm pretty sure I'm falling in love with her mother."

Reagan knew responding to Brett the way she wanted to meant opening herself up to love again and she'd been hurt once before, but this time was different. This time it was a man who'd proved himself. Proved he would put his own reputation in jeopardy to protect her daughter.

She shivered and Brett took off his coat and wrapped it around her shoulders. "See what I mean about feeling safe with you?" she said. "You won't even let me get cold."

Somewhere in New York City a ball dropped, but on the Maine coast, directly above Portland Harbor, fireworks commenced as Brett pulled Reagan close and kissed her ever so gently. "Let's see where this new year takes us," he whispered in her ear.

Reagan could feel herself tearing up, but they were happy tears. It occurred to her in that moment that what had happened in the past no longer mattered. The only thing that mattered now was a new year and a new beginning for her and her daughter…and the man in whose strong arms she felt warm and safe and loved.

About the Author

Rebecca Stevenson is a freelance editor and writer whose frequent visits to New England have become the inspirations and settings for her stories. She is a member of Romance Writers of America and Dallas Area Romance Authors and currently lives in Texas.

Website

http://www.RebeccaStevensonAuthor.com

Made in the USA
Coppell, TX
29 December 2021

70381992R00118